HAWK

Jagged Edge Series #3

A.L. Long

This is a work of fiction. Names, characters, places and incidents either are the product of the author's imagination or used fictionally, and any resemblance to any actual person, living or dead, events or locales is entirely coincidental.

Interior edited by H. Elaine Roughton
Cover design by Laura Sanches

ASIN: B01LXCKOGI
ISBN: 978-1539130703

This book is intended for mature audiences only

Acknowledgment

To my husband of many wonderful years, who has been so supportive of my writing. If it weren't for him my dream of writing would have never been fulfilled. I love you, sweetheart. And to my family, whom I also love dearly. Through their love and support, I can continue my passion for writing.

To the many readers, who took a chance on me and purchased my books. I hope that I can continue to fill your hearts with the passion I have grown to love.

A special thanks to all of the people that supported me at SPS. If you would like to learn about what they can offer you to become a self-publisher, please check out the link below. You will be thankful you did.
https://xe172.isrefer.com/go/curcust/allongbooks

Table of Contents

CHAPTER ONE

Hawk

The last person I expected to hear from was my little brother. So when I got the call that I was needed back home in Stillwater, Oklahoma, I knew that it meant one thing, something was going on with my mom. I left that crappy town for a reason. There wasn't anything left for me there. It had been fifteen years since I'd been back there, except for the last couple of years just to help out my brother or fuck that tight piece of ass who understood my kinky side. My only escape from that shit town was the day I enlisted in the military. My dad, the son of a bitch, said I would never amount to anything. God, how I hated that man. What he did to me and my brother, no child should ever have to go through.

Taking a swig of my brew, I knew I needed to tame down my hatred for the man. Sliding the empty mug to the bartender, I needed something stronger. “Give me a shot of Patron, Kyle,” I said, watching him sanitize the used glasses. I knew my problems weren’t going to disappear with a couple of beers and a few shots. This was about the only way I could deal with what the call from my brother brought. I knew that one day my mom wasn’t going to be able to hold on any longer. That one day was now staring me in the face.

So many times we had pleaded with her to leave him. Joseph Scott Talbott, yeah, major fucking douche bag. Now she is fighting for her life in the nursing home that she spent the last fifteen years in. The last blow almost cost her, her life. She should have died that day, but instead she lives a life with no hope of ever being normal. No hope of ever being able to see, feed herself, dress herself. Just a shell of a woman lying in a bed waiting for the good Lord to take her.

Downing my shot, I twisted in my chair to relieve a few beers. Maybe if I played my cards right, I would get lucky. Getting laid was about the only thing that could suppress my desire to punch someone or something. So when I saw that tight little ass bending over the 20-year-old jukebox, I was all too ready to get me some of that. I only hoped her looks were as nice as her ass.

Putting on my irresistible charm, I walked up behind her and leaned over and casually said, “You know, ‘B14’ is ‘bout the only song worth a shit listening to.”

When her eyes met mine, I could tell her interest was more than I wanted to give her. I didn’t have time for a long relationship, I was the one night stand kind of guy. ‘Fuck ‘em and forget ‘em’ was my motto.

Taking in her smile, I knew it wasn’t meant for me. Following the gaze of her eyes, I could see a pretty good-sized guy heading our way. My potential one night stand just turned into a potential fight that I didn’t want any part of. Backing away, I headed down the short hallway and slipped into the men’s bathroom. As luck would have it, I was the only one in the small room that could have used a cleaning crew. Getting rid of a few brews, I thought about all the shit that would be waiting for me in Oklahoma. I hated dealing with that shit, it was one of the reasons I didn't argue when Drew requested to be the executor of my mom's estate. That bullshit wasn't for me. My little bro was better at handling that stuff. He was the one with the business degree.

As I left the bathroom, I could see that my little angel was sitting by herself at the bar. I thought it odd since her shadow made it perfectly clear that she was taken. Pulling a chair up beside her, I flagged Kyle to get me another Patron and a cold one. I thought now was as good a time as any to find out what the deal was with this chick. "So your boyfriend left you alone?"

Looking over my way with those baby blues, she said, "He isn't my boyfriend, even though he would like to think he is."

That little tidbit of information sent a rush of hope to the tip of my cock. "Seemed pretty attached to you."

"Yeah, well, he's not," she confirmed, taking a sip

of her fruity something or another.

" Can I buy you a drink?" I asked, knowing it was the oldest pick-up line, but still worked like a charm.

"Sure," she nodded, "Tequila Sunrise, please."

Looking over to her with a smile, I realized that I could no more fuck this creature than I could my own sister if I had one. There was something about her that was innocent. Running my hand through my hair, I downed the rest of my drink and said, "Catch you later, doll."

"Yeah, sure. Thanks for the drink," she said, holding up her Sunrise.

~****~

Getting to my place, I threw the keys to my Mustang on the counter and headed to the fridge to see what I could find to eat. The only thing that looked even remotely edible was a slice of pizza from two nights ago. Forgoing heating it up, I grabbed a napkin and took a seat on the leather couch. Even though my place wasn't big, it suited me just fine. I had a great view of the city, it was in the nicer part of Manhattan, and it had all the amenities that I needed. Couch, plasma TV, one bedroom with a connecting bathroom, and an office to do all my business stuff. Perfect. Bachelor pad at its finest.

Pushing from the couch, I grabbed a glass of water and headed to bed. If I wanted to get to Oklahoma at a reasonable time, I would need to get some sleep. It was a drive I wasn't looking forward to making. Just as I was ready to settle in my cold king-sized bed, my cell began to ring.

Looking down at the screen, I answered in annoyance, "I was just about ready to turn in. Do you know what time it is?"

"Sorry, bro. I thought I'd let you know they don't expect Ma to make it past tomorrow night. Just thought you might want to know," Drew said.

"Fuck, I'll be there as soon as I can," I said,

between gritted teeth.

Grabbing my duffel bag from my closet, I began throwing everything I could think of inside. These were not the plans I had for tonight. It was late and I wasn't exactly in the right frame of mind to be traveling the twenty-two hours it was going to take me to get to Stillwater. With everything in hand, I left my cozy home and headed to the street where my car was parked. Getting to my car, I threw my stuff in the trunk and got in. As I started the engine, I could see that there was something placed on the windshield under the wiper. "God, are you fucking serious?" I said out loud as I opened the door and leaned over to grab the yellow ticket. *What the hell, don't those damn meter maids ever sleep?*

Shoving the ticket in my glove box, I put the car in drive and pulled away from the curb. Even though it was still light out, I could feel the difference in the air. The days were getting shorter and the nights were getting colder. Fall was right around the corner. As I pulled out of the city onto I-80, my phone began to vibrate. Pressing the 'hands free' on the steering wheel, I listened for Peter to say something.

"Hey, Hawk, have you left the city yet?" Peter asked.

"Just heading out now. What's up?" I asked.

"Just wanted to wish you the best and to have a safe trip," Peter paused. "I almost forgot to tell you, Cop and Brie announced their wedding plans, they are looking at an October 25th wedding. Make sure you mark your calender."

"Thanks for the info. I'll call you when I get to Stillwater." As I hung up the phone all I could think about was how happy Cop was. How he managed to find the woman of his dreams, and how fucked up it was for me to even think about finding that. Peter, Cop, and the rest of the guys at Jagged Edge Security were the closest thing I had to a family other than my brother Drew. The day that Peter asked me to be a part of his team, I was all in.

~****~

I had been driving for about four hours and I needed to get some fuel and stretch my legs. Maybe even grab something to eat. Pulling into the gas station, I filled my tank and watched as the cars passed by on the street. Returning the gas nozzle back to its cradle, I noticed an attractive, brown haired, blue-eyed babe getting harassed by a couple of punks. Locking my car, I stepped over to where she was having a hard time getting gas in her little beat-up Honda Civic.

Getting between her and the two guys, I took the gas nozzle from her and looked her in the eye. “Hey, doll, these guys giving you trouble?”

“I’m good,” she said, taking hold of the nozzle and continuing to pump the gas into her car.

Turning to the two guys that were standing on the other side of the gas island, I watched them walk away from the truck they were driving and head to the small store. Looking back over my shoulder, I could see that my blue-eyed babe was rounding the car and getting in. Jogging to her side, I held her door open and asked with a smile, “So, what is your name, doll?”

“It is definitely not ‘doll,’” she said.

“Okay, then what?” I replied.

“See you around,” she stated as she turned the key in her ignition and grabbed for the door handle.

What a surprise, I had never been brushed off by a woman before in my life. They were either begging me to fuck them or to at least give me head, but there was something different about that girl. She made the chase that much more worthwhile.

CHAPTER TWO

Paige

I wasn't sure who that guy thought he was, but I was in no mood for his alpha-male shit. Why is it that every guy who is drop-dead gorgeous thinks that they can get any woman that they want? Even though he was gorgeous and he had a body made of steel, there was no way I was about to give him the time of day. Besides, who uses the word 'doll' as a come-on anymore?

As I drove down the highway, I knew I needed to speed it up a little if I was going to make it to Stillwater, Oklahoma, in time. It wasn't one of my top choices of places I wanted to live, but I knew small towns tended to go unnoticed, and right now, I really needed to stay that way. The only thing left to do was make sure that I got the job at the only hopping bar in the little town. When my only friend in New York told me about 'Hell's Gate,' and that they were looking for a bartender, I knew it was the only opportunity I had to get out of New York and have a job lined up for me somewhere else. Constantly being on the run was beginning to take a toll on me. Over the past twelve months I had lived in eight different cities and had just as many jobs.

Putting my old beater in drive, I pulled away from the gas pump and made my way back onto I-80. *"Here we come, Stillwater,"* I said to myself as I placed my ten dollar sunglasses over my eyes. Lost in my thoughts, I kept considering how things could have turned out differently had my uncle just agreed to let me stay in the States and continue my Masters at NYU. But he didn't, he said that I had an obligation to Kierabali and its people.

The thing was, I didn't want to go back. I knew what was waiting for me. A man I had never met, a wedding of the century, and a life filled with only sadness and loneliness. At least here in the States, I got to make my own choices. I got to choose where I lived, where I worked, who my friends were, and most of all, I got to choose who I would be marrying. So the minute the opportunity came, I escaped. Even though it was my birthright, I had nothing more there. My parents were gone and the only person left was my uncle, Maxwell, who I couldn't care less about. As far as I was concerned, he could run the tiny country himself.

Trying to focus on the road, I heard a loud pop, which sound like it was coming from the back of the car. Pulling to the side of the road, I turned off the car and opened the door. There it was, as plain as day, a flat tire. "Shit! Shit! Shit!" I yelled out, knowing that no one would be able to hear me. Popping open the trunk, I grabbed what looked to be some sort of wrench and a small jack. I knew that there had to be a spare tire somewhere in there. It was then I saw the hidden compartment on the bottom of the trunk. Sure enough, there it was. Only the tire was about half the size of a normal tire. The problem was, I wasn't sure how to put it on and take the other one off. Certainly there had to be instructions on how to change a tire.

Walking to the front passenger side of the car, I

fumbled through the glove box to see if I could find the owner's manual. I bought this car at one of those mom and pop car dealers. It was the only car that I was able to pay cash for. Having no luck finding the owner's manual. I closed the door to find that a black Mustang pulled in behind me. The guy driving was the last person that I wanted to see. Heading to my trunk to get the tire out, I was met with the hard build of Mr. Alpha-Male Gorgeousness.

"Let me help you with that," he said as he took hold of the tire and pulled it out of the trunk like it was nothing.

"Um… I can get this myself. It's not like I don't know what I'm doing," I said, hoping he didn't see right through my lie.

"By all means, go ahead," he commanded, leaning his body against the side of the car.

Taking hold of the X-shaped wrench, I walked over to the flat tire and stared at it. I wasn't sure what to do with the wrench. There were no bolts to loosen. I had no idea where to even start. Hot-to-Trot must have seen my reluctance because he placed his hand on my shoulder, which sent a fire through my body, and took the wrench from me. With expertise, he lowered his body to a squatting position and took the flat end of the wrench and slid it between the rim and the hub cap. With a flick of his wrist the cap was off, exposing five bolts.

I felt like a total idiot. It took him less than fifteen minutes to change the tire, throw the flat in the trunk, and shut the lid, handing me my keys that I left in the lock. He smiled down on me and said, "Here you go, doll. You will need to get a real tire on that. It should hold you for about fifty miles."

Taking the keys, I felt a tingling in my inner thighs, making its way to my soaked panties. It was only when I saw those magnificent hazel eyes that the words left my head. While I stood there like a fool drooling all over him, he placed his hand on my shoulder and turned my body towards the front of the car. With a little slap to my ass, he leaned over and whispered, "Off you go," before he walked back to his car.

~****~

Seeing a gas station about ten miles from where I had my encounter with Mr. Hot Stuff, I pulled into the station and headed towards the service garage. Most of the guys inside were working on motors and wearing grease-covered overalls. I could smell the gas and oil odor as I walked to the door that said 'Office.' Knocking lightly, I heard a gruff voice on the other side say, "Enter."

I wasn't sure what to expect, but when an older bald-headed gentleman looked up at me, I thought I was going to die right then and there. Not only was his head as bald as could be, but a long scar ran from the top of his left brow, down the side of his face, and curved just before it disappeared under his chin. Holding my composure, I said in a stern tone, "I have a tire that I need to get replaced."

When he looked up at me like I was out of my mind, I knew that my tire wasn't going to be getting fixed anytime soon. "Ma'am, we are kinda busy here. Could be a while. There's a diner up the street if you want to wait."

"How long are we talking? I need to get on the road," I said, frustrated.

"At least a couple of hours. You take your pretty little self to the diner, I'll have one of my guys come getcha when it's done," he said as he picked his teeth with a toothpick.

After I left the service station, I did as the mechanic suggested and headed to the small diner. It didn't look like much on the outside, but sometimes looks could be deceiving. Walking up the wooden steps, I swung open the door and was met by the scent of cinnamon and coffee. Whatever it was, I knew that was what I wanted.

Sitting at the counter, which reminded me of a 1950's burger joint, I watched a younger waitress take an order from a customer sitting on the other end. One thing that I had to say, the little pink uniform was kind of cute on her, especially with the silk yellow daisy pinned to her lapel. Looking down at the menu, I looked for anything that was made with cinnamon. As I skimmed over the dessert section, there it was, 'Grandma's Old-Fashioned Cinnamon

Rolls.' Placing the menu on the counter, I waited for the waitress to finish up with her customer.

As I waited, I took in my surroundings. The little diner was definitely like something out of the fifties. The booths were red with white tables. Even the bar seat I was sitting on was red. There was also an old jukebox in the corner, which was playing 'Johnny Angel.' I also noticed that the curtains were red checkered and the floor was black and white tiled. Nothing like being sent back in time.

"Are you ready to order?" the waitress asked as she poured me a glass of water.

"Yeah," I said, picking up the menu.

Once my order was placed, I pulled out my phone and began looking at the pictures I had taken of my friend in New York. God, how much I missed her. I wished I didn't have to leave my job and my friend. But when the strange calls began to happen, I knew that they had found me. My only option was to find a different place to live and dump my phone and get a new one. Knowing my uncle, he would be tracking my every move. I couldn't risk him finding me.

While I was lost in looking at my pictures, the young waitress came back with my order. Placing my phone on the counter, I looked down at the cinnamon roll and licked my lips in delight. It was a gooey, ooey, mess of perfection with caramel running over the edge and walnuts following its trail. When the first bite hit my mouth, I knew I was in heaven. Little old grandma really outdid herself with this recipe. It didn't take long before the last bite was down. Picking up my phone to check the time, I heard the little bell above the door chime. Looking over my shoulder, I saw one of the men from the garage. Throwing a ten on the counter, I twisted in my chair and walked over to the man in greasy overalls.

"Hey, Dex, can I get you anything?" the waitress asked as she picked up my empty plate.

"I'm good, Abby," he said.

The waitress smiled at him and headed to the

kitchen. Turning my attention back to the mechanic, I asked, “Is my tire fixed?”

“All done and ready to go,” he said.

As he held the door open, I stepped in front of him and headed back to the garage. I was so glad that it didn’t take the two hours the other mechanic thought it would. As much as I enjoyed this quaint little town, I needed to get going. The last thing I wanted was to be late for my first day on the job.

CHAPTER THREE

Hawk

How can a woman I hardly know have such an effect on me? My dick had never been so hard. I never thought the day would come where a woman would be immune to my charm. But that woman, she was like no one I had ever met. Not only was she beautiful, she had a cheeky side that I found sexy as hell. Normally it would have been a turn-off for me, but holy hell, wow.

Pulling into Stillwater, I could see that nothing had changed since the last time I was here. Just a lot of bad memories that I chose to forget. Even the 'Welcome to Stillwater' sign didn't change. The old bell tower that was built when I was a kid still had the same pewter statue of some historical founder of the town or some shit like that.

Even though I had never been to the nursing home that my mom was in, I knew exactly where it was. Driving up the street, I noticed another thing that never changed. It was the old men sitting in front of the only diner that was worth a shit, rocking on the wooden chairs that were older than dirt.

Turning off the main street, the nursing home came into view. Even though I had never been here, there was something about the place that gave me a somber feeling. It was the last place most of the people went to until the good Lord took them. I think I would kill myself first before I lived in a place like this. Depending on someone to wipe my ass was not what I envisioned my older age would consist of. I hoped that when the time came for me to go, I would die quickly and painlessly.

Pulling the Mustang into the parking lot, I turned off the engine and headed to the front entrance. As I walked up the sidewalk, there were several residents sitting in wheelchairs with their heads hung low. Yeah, this was definitely not the life I want for myself. Passing the path of the sleeping, I swung open the entrance door.

Scoping out the area, I spotted a nurse's station to the right of the entrance. There were two women dressed in colorful scrub tops sitting behind the counter, one older and one much younger. Leaning against the countertop, I asked, "Can you let me know which room Nadine Talbott is in?"

The older one looked up and asked, "And you are?"

"My name is Jayce Talbott. I'm her older son," I replied with a smile.

My smile must have warmed her cold heart, because I could see a hint of a smile cross her face. "Mrs. Talbott is in room 102. Straight down the hall and to the left."

As I headed that way, I wondered what I would find once I entered her room. By the way my brother spoke, she didn't have too much time left. Just as I was getting ready to enter her room, a man dressed in a black shirt with a white collar exited. When I looked at him, I knew that I was too late. Stepping past him, I entered the room to find that Drew was leaning over my mother's body, with his hand placed on her.

Stepping closer, I placed my hand on his shoulder, letting him know that I was here. He didn't even look at me as he choked, "She didn't make it, Jayce. She held on as long as she could."

I could tell by the sound of his voice that it really affected him. I stepped beside him and looked down at the woman that used to be my mother. Her body was gray and lifeless. Going by the way she looked, she had been struggling for some time. Her cheeks were sunk in and her hands were paper thin. When Drew told me that she would be spending the rest of her life under the care of a nursing facility, I had no idea how bad she really was. God, what a stupid woman she was. If she had just listened to me when I told her to get away from my father, she might still be alive. But, at least now she will be at peace. No one will ever hurt her again.

~****~

By the time we filled out the necessary paperwork,

it was close to eight o'clock. Drew and I decided to meet up in the morning to work out the details of the funeral arrangements. This was the part where I had no problem with Drew planning the whole damn thing. For one thing, I wasn't much on funerals, and for another, planning them was one thing I knew nothing about.

The one thing I did know was where the bar was. Getting in my car, I turned on the engine and headed to a brew that had my name on it. I would have invited my brother to go with me, but I knew he wanted to get home to his perfect family. Never quite understood why he married a woman he barely knew only because he felt it was his obligation as a gentleman, seeing as he knocked her up.

Hell's Gate was already in full swing when I pulled up to the best bar in this little town. I will never forget the first time I came here. I was only seventeen, with a fake ID my friend Jimmy managed to get his hands on. It was supposed to be the last hurrah before I went off into the service. Only my last hurrah ended up being my first fight over a damn girl who was four years older than me. That was the day I decided to ward off women completely. Well, not completely. A man still had needs.

As I opened the door, I could smell the scent of liquor and cigarette smoke in the air. Stepping up to the bar, I asked what they had on draft and scanned the room while I waited for my beer. My eyes were glued to the vision at the end of the bar. There she was, Ms. Sassy Pants herself. It should have been illegal, the way she bent over to pick up the case of beer. I had never been so turned on by looking at a sweet little ass like the one she had. All I could imagine was how it would feel to press that tight ass against my hard cock.

Taking a swig of my beer, I watched as she maneuvered between a couple of guys standing at the end of the bar. One thing I had to say, she sure did know how to carry a case of beer bottles. I just about lost it when she pushed the swinging door at the end of the bar with her butt. Man, oh man, did I ever need relief, but there was no way I was going to move and miss out on the show I was watching. Even the way she was stacking the bottles in the cooler had me turned on. Her sizable breasts peeking out under her tank top had me wanting to put my hands over them and caress them to no end.

When she looked up, her eyes met mine like a lightning bolt. I had never seen anything like it. The way the dim lights caught them, I swore they were made of glass. Like a shimmering light bouncing off of the blue sea. But what got me most, was the look she was giving me. I wasn't sure if it was a look of delight or disgust. Whatever it was, she had me, hook, line, and sinker. With her hands on her hips, she walked over to where I was sitting. I knew then that the look she was giving me was a look of anger, but I had no clue as to why.

"Are you some kind of stalker or something?" she asked as she crossed her arms in front of her chest.

"Don't get your lacy panties in a wad, doll. I grew up here and my mom just passed, so give a guy a little break," I replied.

"Oh, God, I'm so sorry. I thought… never mind what I thought. My name is Paige," she said, holding out her hand.

"It's okay, my mom and I weren't close. I'm Hawk, by the way."

"Well, it's nice to meet you, Hawk. Can I buy you another beer?"

"Yeah, but only if you promise to have one with me."

"I can't drink on the job, but I get a break in about fifteen minutes, we could maybe talk then."

With all the shit that happened today, it was beginning to look up. The girl who had me all hot and bothered for the last 24 hours finally had a name. The best part being, I might actually get the chance to get to know her better. Downing the rest of my beer, I headed to the men's room to drain the beast. As I was going in, a dude was coming out. He had no regard for me as he bumped right into me. I knew that he may have had a little too much to drink by the way he was staggering to get past me. It wasn't until I looked him straight in the eye that I recognized him. He didn't change a bit over the last fifteen years. The only difference was that he was a little taller and a little stockier. He must not have recognized me though, because no sooner than his eyes met mine, they were focused on Paige, who was pouring drinks.

As I grabbed his arm, I said, “If it isn’t Bobby Brennan. How the hell are you?”

“Who the hell are you, fucker?” he asked, glaring at me with bloodshot eyes.

“Jayce Talbott. I take it you don’t recognize me. Remember, I’m the one who planted a fist in your gut before we got kicked out of here some fifteen years ago,” I reminded him.

There must have been something in what I said, because in an instant he suddenly became sober. “Yeah, I remember you,” he paused, looking me over. “You ruined my fucking life that day.”

Bobby pulled his arm from my grasp. I thought he was going to explain to me how the hell *I* managed to ruin his life all those years ago, when he clearly was well on his way to doing that all by himself. Bobby was the biggest bully in Stillwater. Everyone did what he asked in fear that they would be getting their ass kicked if they didn't. The day me and my friend Jimmy got in Hell's Gate was the day that I finally got enough nerve to stand up to him. It only took that one punch to the gut and he was down. I must have hit him just right, because it took him a long time to get off the floor. By the time he finally did, Jimmy and I were already escorted out of the bar and on our way. We never knew what happened to him after that. I left the next day for the military and Jimmy later moved upstate to help his uncle with his landscaping business. Never heard from either of them again.

"How the hell did I ruin your life? If I recall, you were an asshole back then," I clarified.

"Yeah, well, ever since that day, no one wants anything to do with me. I can't even get a decent job," he said.

"Oh come on, Bobby. There is no way my hitting

you in the stomach caused all the problems you're having."

"I should just clock you right now and get it over with. You're lucky, I've had too much to drink."

As Bobby walked away, there was something about him that didn't seem right. I would never believe he would back down from a fight because he may have had a little too much to drink. Not thinking any more about it, I turned to the bathroom door to take care of business.

CHAPTER FOUR

Paige

I wasn't sure what I was getting myself into, but there was something about that man that had my panties wet. Offering to have a little chat with him during my break didn't mean that I was going to jump his bones. It was the last thing I wanted to do or could afford to do. But holy Jesus, he was hot. And that smile of his just about made me explode on the spot. Whenever I felt a guy get remotely close to me, I usually put on the bitch attitude, hoping that they would get the picture that I wasn't interested, but with this guy things were different. There was some thing about him that I couldn't get my mind off of.

My friend was right about this bar. Even though it was situated in a small town, it was the hot spot. I couldn't believe how quickly the bar filled within a matter of hours. It wasn't even a Friday night. I should have known when the owner said, "Hope you're up for a killer night," he wanted to make sure that I would be prepared to run my ass off. So when my break came, I was more than ready to rest my feet.

Grabbing a diet coke, I walked over to where Hawk was sitting sipping his draft beer. Pulling up the chair beside him, I felt his eyes burning into me. Looking over to him with a confused look I said, "What?"

With the touch of his hand, he swiped a stray piece of hair behind my ear that escaped from my loose pony. His touch was so tender, And God, there was that smile again. Taking a sip of my coke, I looked down the bar and asked, "How come you are in a bar instead of mourning your mom's death?"

"Long story," he said.

"I'd love to hear it, but I have to get back to work. Maybe we can grab a coffee when I get off," I suggested.

"Yeah, sure."

I wasn't sure what possessed me to be so bold. I had never asked a guy for anything. Pushing from the bar, I picked up my empty glass of coke and took my place behind the bar knowing that every move I made, Hawk's eyes were peeled to my backside, which was one of my best assets if I had to say so myself.

As the night wore on, the bar was now standing room only, I knew there was an occupancy law being broken. The local Fire Marshal would have a heyday with this one if he came in to do an inspection. With the amount of people in the bar, I was also surprised to see that there weren't too many fights. With all the male testosterone inside, Bucky, the bouncer only had to escort a handful of guys out. It always seemed there was a girl involved. That didn't surprise me either, considering the population of men to women was two to one.

By the time last call came, I was ready to die. My feet had never hurt so bad. Even though I wasn't new to the hard work that came with slinging drinks, I had never worked so hard in my life. If it was going to be busy like this every night, I needed to think about wearing something different on my feet. My cute sandals were not going to cut it.

Hawk was sitting patiently at the end of the bar while I finished loading the coolers with beer. Bucky had already left, and Merrill, the owner, was in his office counting his profits for the evening. I knew he made out pretty good based on my tip jar, which was overflowing with money.

Wiping off the bar, I stepped over to Hawk and asked, “You ready for that coffee?”

“Yes, ma’am,” he replied with that gorgeous smile.

Folding the bar towel in half and draping it over the faucet, I rounded the bar and took Hawk by the hand. His hand was so big that I wasn’t able to get mine around it, but he got the hint that I wanted him to follow me. It was three o’clock in the morning and the local diner where most of the customers went after the bar closed didn’t seem to be the best place to talk. Even though I didn't know him very well, I was pretty sure it was safe to invite him to my place for coffee.

As we walked to the back of the bar, I could tell that Hawk was wondering where I was leading him. Looking over my shoulder I said, "I live above the bar. It's small, but it is nice.

"Lead the way, then," he replied.

Leading him, we exited through the back door and headed up the stairs on the outside of the building. Having to exit the bar to get to my apartment was something that I wished was different. The lighting wasn't very good. The only light was from the lamp I placed on a small table in front of the window. It was better than not having any light at all. Alleys were like a magnet, drawing in weird people. Reaching in my pocket, I pulled out my key to open the door.

When I told Merrill that I needed to find a place to live, he offered me the tiny apartment above the bar. He said it wasn't much, but the rent was cheap and it was clean. He was right, it was perfect for me. The one-bedroom apartment was small. It had a tiny kitchen that opened up to the living room, which was big enough for only a couch and a chair. The bedroom wasn't much bigger, but at least it had a queen-sized bed, a dresser, and best of all, an attached bathroom. I also liked that it had a big window in the living room that overlooked the small town.

As I closed the door, I turned to Hawk and said, "Make yourself at home. I'll put on a pot of coffee."

"Sounds good," he said, taking a seat on the couch.

Pulling the coffee from the cupboard and placing a couple of heaping scoops in the paper filter, I filled the pot with water and then poured it in the top. Once I could see that the coffee was beginning to brew, I made my way over to where Hawk was sitting. I guess I didn't realize how big he actually was. The way he was sitting on my couch, it made it look smaller than it actually was. His body was leaning forward with his elbows resting on his lap and his hands crossed between them. Feeling the need to keep my distance, I sat in the small chair beside the couch.

Crossing my legs Indian style, I glanced over to him, and asked, “So you said that your mom died, that must be really hard for you.”

“Nah. My mom and I weren’t very close. I’m mostly here for my little brother,” he confessed.

“What, happened… to your mom?”

“She just made some choices that in the end cost her her life. Can’t change the past.”

I got the feeling that Hawk wasn’t willing to share with me why he and his mom weren’t close. I didn’t want to pry into his personal life. It wasn’t because I didn’t want to know more about him, it was because I didn’t want him asking questions of mine. Even though I had already made up a fairy tale story, I needed to be careful with how much I shared. Hearing the beep on the coffee maker, I pushed from my chair and headed back towards the kitchen.

Pulling two mugs from the cupboard, I looked over to him and asked, "Do you take anything in your coffee? Milk? Sugar?"

"Nah, just black," he stated.

Doctoring my own coffee, I walked with both cups in hand to where he was sitting. Handing him his cup, I felt the brush of his hand over mine. It amazed me how a big alpha-male type could have such a soft touch. His hand lingered over mine a little longer than needed, but I didn't mind. It was only after he removed his hand from mine that I diverted my gaze elsewhere.

Leaving his side, I took my place once again in the little chair. Just as I was about to sit, I heard him ask, "So what in the hell brought you to Stillwater?"

Taking a deep breath, I began to explain. "Just needed a change. I love New York, but it was getting too mundane."

“So of all places you could go, you chose Stillwater. This town is as unexciting as you can get,” he stated.

“Yeah, but it’s different, I have to at least give it a chance.”

Shaking his head, I could see that either he didn’t believe me or thought I was crazy. “You know, not everybody comes to Stillwater for a change. It’s not exactly the place that would come up if you Googled small towns. So there has to be another reason,” he argued.

“Well, my friend back in New York knew that I wanted a change and she told me about this place. She said they were looking for a good bartender. So I just went for it. I thought what the hell,” I said, hoping it would satisfy his question.

“So, I need to ask, I sense a hint of an accent in your voice, Can I ask where you are from?” Hawk asked.

“Shit, shit, shit,” I thought to myself. I had been trying so hard to change my voice so that my accent

wouldn't be noticed. I wasn't sure what to tell him. So I just went with the first thing that came to mind. "I don't think I have an accent. Maybe it comes from being everywhere. I traveled a lot when I was a kid."

"So was your dad in the military or something?" he askcd.

"Not exactly. How about a refill?" I asked, rising to my feet, knowing I needed to get away from this conversation.

"Nah, I'm good," he said as he walked up behind me.

I could feel the heat in my body rise the closer he got. If he got any closer, I knew I would spontaneously combust. His scent was indescribable, the way it filled the space between us. The tingle between my legs was growing and the wetness there was beginning to emerge. When he placed his hands on my shoulders, I just about lost it. It was the softest touch I had ever felt.

When I turned my body to face him, his hand caressed my cheek lightly until it was replaced with a light kiss. My eyes closed, taking in the feel of him being so close to me. It wasn't until his lips touched mine that I fell apart. The strength of his arms wrapped around me as our kiss deepened. A shallow moan escaped my mouth, sending a vibration between our entwined tongues. Everything inside me was telling me to back away from him, but I couldn't move. All I wanted was to feel more of what he was giving. His hands traced the curve of my ass before he had me lifted from the tile floor. It didn't take long for my legs to wrap around his waist. Trailing kisses along my jaw line to the base of my neck, his assault on my body continued.

There was nothing more that I wanted to do but take him in. My head fell back, soaking in the tenderness of his soft lips on my skin. One kiss after the other, he trailed them down my body, stopping at the top of my chest where the point of no return was waiting to be explored. As much as I wanted to tell him to stop, my body was telling him, "Please don't quit." Lifting me high enough, he gently placed my ass on the counter. Working his hands up my body, they found their place at the hem of my t-shirt before he lifted it up and off of me. My breathing was deep, waiting for his next move.

With a gentle touch, Hawk placed his hand on my cheek and said softly, "I am going to have to fuck you, doll, and just to let you know, 'no' is not an option."

Even if I could tell him no, there was no way I would ever want to. Taking my hands in his, he took me by my wrists and placed them behind my back, causing my breasts to push forward. While one hand had a hold of my wrist behind my back, the other expertly unfastened the front clasp of my bra. My breasts fell free and were exposed, pert and ready to be consumed. Hawk's mouth lowered to the sensitized nipple of my right breast, which caused my head to tip backwards. The way he worked his tongue, sucking and licking the hard bud, was unlike anything I had ever felt before. While his lips were toying with my sensitized nipples, his hands found the top button of my shorts. Lifting my butt off of the counter, he pulled them down my thighs until they landed on the hard floor.

The lace of my sexy thong snapped as he took the fragile material between his fingers and ripped them off. His animalistic manner set my body soaring as he brought them to his nose and breathed in my scent and then stuffed the shattered lace in his pocket. With a mischievous grin, he whispered in my ear, “Are you ready to be fucked, doll?”

Those weren’t the words that I had expected and I wasn’t sure if I was ready to be taken by this man. Even though I wasn’t a virgin, the one and only time I had ever had sex wasn’t a memory I wanted to remember. If my parents ever knew how I lost my virginity, they would be rolling in their graves. As my thoughts drifted, Hawk’s hands also did. His movement was so quick that I didn’t have time to think before he had my body turned and bent over the small counter. I could feel the hardness of his cock as he pushed it against my bare ass. The way he pressed against me, I knew it would just be a matter of time before he would be filling me, coating his shaft with my wetness.

I heard the sound of his zipper before his pants fell to the floor. As he leaned closer to my ear, he once again confessed his intentions, "God, you are so wet, beautiful, and the sight of your pretty little ass has me so hard that I can already feel your tight pussy."

"What are you waiting for?" I asked, knowing if he didn't take me soon, I would be unleashing my arousal any second just from his commanding voice.

Closing my eyes, I felt the tip of his cock gliding up and down my slick folds. Just when I thought he was ready to plunge deep inside, he pulled away and said, "Hold tight, baby."

Standing with my legs parted and my upper body leaning over the counter, I looked behind me to see that be was bent over with his jeans in his hands, searching for what I could only assume was a condom. I was thankful that he was at least smart enough to protect us from an unnecessary mistake. Hearing the rip of the wrapper, I settled back on the counter and waited for him to roll it on.

When I looked back over to him, my eyes were automatically drawn to the size of his cock. I took a deep breath, knowing that I might not be able to fully take him. And that it was going to hurt, especially having been without sex for so long. Focusing on him, I watched as he gently took hold of my hip and pulled my body closer to his. "Lift up to your toes, baby," I heard him request behind me.

Placing my palms on the cold counter, I braced myself as I rose to my tiptoes. The position of his cock and the added height of my ass allowed him to enter me. The pressure of his impressive cock pushing inside me was almost too much to handle. I wanted to push against him, but knew that I needed to take this slow. "God damn, baby girl, you are so tight," he confessed as he continued his slow movements inside me.

If he only knew that he was only the second man that I had been with. Actually, I would have to say the first one, considering my first time was with a boy. A small moan radiated through my lips as he pushed even deeper inside my tight channel. With one hand on my leg, he moved the other to my breast. With him tweaking my nipple between his fingers, my release came before he fully entered me. It had been so long, my body could no longer hold on. “Holy fuck, darlin’, you feel so fuckin’ good,” he said.

Hawk’s hand wandered up my body, following the curve of my spine before it settled where my loose pony was. With one tug of my hair tie, my hair fell on my shoulders as he raked his fingers through the long locks. Tipping my head back, he whispered in my ear. “Please tell me you’ve been fucked before?”

With a deep sigh, I muttered, “Once,” hoping that my confession wouldn’t make him stop.

“Well, my dick loves your tight pussy,” he said.

“Well, my pussy loves your big dick.” I normally wouldn’t be talking so boldly, but the way I was feeling, I knew I was bound to have another orgasm before he had his first.

Even though the grip he had on my hair was causing me a little discomfort, the pleasure he was giving me outweighed it ten to one. The harder he pulled my head back, using it as a way to push deeper inside me, the fuller I became. It was only after he thrust one last time that I knew he met his own release. Loosening the grip he had on my head, his body relaxed and cradled mine. His palms took their place next to mine before he placed them on top. It was an affectionate move on his part, and was quickly lost when he pulled from me, leaving me wanting more.

"I need to get out of here, busy day tomorrow," he admitted.

Before I could protest, he was out the door, with no other indication that he would see me tomorrow or that he even wanted to. It didn't matter because I knew the drill. 'Fuck 'em and forget 'em.' Typical male. I always managed to find them. Either that, or they knew how to spot a desperate girl. This was the main reason for my bitchy attitude. If they thought for one second that you were unobtainable, you wouldn't need to worry about them coming on to you. Silly me, how could I have possibly thought that this guy was any different.

Grabbing what was left of my clothes, I headed to the bathroom to take a much needed shower. I needed to wash the guilt I was feeling off of my body. It wasn't because I felt guilty for having sex with a man I hardly knew. It was because I just got used.

CHAPTER FIVE

Hawk

I felt like such an ass. I'd been so used to one night stands that I did the one thing I had always done, get a good fuck and hightail it out of there before they started getting all clingy and shit. It was my way, only this time, I felt like shit. The look on Paige's face said it all. As soon as I closed that door behind me, I knew she was hurt. I should have turned back and knocked on her door and explained. Instead, I walked away.

Getting in my Mustang, I drove up the main street until I came upon a place I thought I would never come back to. Pulling up to the curb, I looked over to the small house that now had boarded up windows and a big sign on the door that I assumed said, "Condemned. No trespassing.'

A home that should have been filled with love and happiness. Only this house was filled with pain and sadness. A whole lot of pain.

Reaching for the door handle, I opened the door and headed towards the rundown house. As I rounded the car, I remembered I had a flashlight in the glove box. Unlocking the door, I reached inside and popped open the glove compartment. Pulling the flashlight out, I relocked the door and walked across the street to the small house. The grass had been overtaken by weeds that must have been at least a foot high. You would have thought that the city would have at least mowed them down to keep the appearance of the town looking like they gave a damn.

As I walked up the slanted steps, which I thought for sure were going to split in two, I looked around to make sure there wasn't anyone else around. The last thing I needed was to get caught being somewhere I wasn't supposed to be. Walking across the rickety porch, I looked between the boards that had been nailed across the windows. Unable to see anything, I jumped off the end of the wooden platform and headed to the back of the house. It was then that I remembered the basement window my brother and I used to sneak out of. It was the only window that there wasn't a lock on, at least one that worked. Crouching down on my haunches, I pulled hard on the window a few times until it finally opened. Rolling over to my stomach, I began inching my way through the small window. It was much easier getting in through the window some fifteen years ago than it was now. I guess I should have taken that into account before I attempted to fit through the small space. Turning my shoulders at an angle, I was finally able to squeeze my body in. Landing on an old box, I lowered myself to the concrete floor.

The musty smell along with the rancid smell of dry blood hit me. I knew it was mine, to be exact. Reaching up to the window, I pulled it closed to make sure there was no sign that someone had entered. I began taking the steps to the main floor as slowly as possible. Who knew how stable the wooden steps would be after all these years? The last thing I wanted was to die in this shit hole. Safely at the top of the stairs, I looked to the heavens and thanked God I made it. Opening the door, I heard the familiar sound of the door creak. It didn't matter how much grease I put on that damn door, it never stopped creaking.

The house was completely dark, so I twisted the head of the flashlight until the light came on. From the looks of everything, it seemed like most of the fixtures from the old house had been stripped off the walls and ceiling. On some of the walls, colorful graffiti had been painted on them that had to have taken a lot of time to paint. Some of them were quite good. It made me wonder what else went on in this house besides abuse and neglect. Based on the amount of art on the walls, I would speculate that gang members took over the house until it was seized by the government.

There were so many bad memories in this house, I wasn't even sure what the hell I was doing here. I guess in the back of my mind, I was punishing myself for the way things turned out for me. Even though my attitude changed once I enlisted, there was still one thing that didn't, and that was the way I treated women. Maybe I was more like my dad than I wanted to admit. After everything he did to my mom, you would think I would never want to be like him. He hit her so many times when I was a kid. I remembered every single one of them, only because every time I tried to stop him, I got it as well, only worse. Every fist that came in contact with my body made me hate my mom more and more. Instead of taking us away from that shit, she just took it day after day. I thought for sure that after the dozens of times she ended up in the hospital, she had enough and would finally leave.

It was only after I ended up in the ER that she finally said, “No More,” only it was too late. It was the final blow to her head that landed her in that care facility. She could have had so much, but she chose pain over happiness.

Wandering down the hall, I came upon the room that Drew and I shared. The only things left were the faded stains on the wallpaper where our posters and his awards used to hang. Shining the light on the closet door, I gripped the knob and swung the door open. Pointing the light to the ceiling, I saw the entrance to the attic. Spotting a milk crate in the corner of the room, I grabbed it and placed it on the floor in the closet. Stepping on it, I pushed the small cover in the ceiling up and over, giving me the room I needed. I reached inside the hole, feeling for the one thing I knew would still be there. Pulling out the tattered backpack covered in dust, I slung it over my shoulder and got the hell out of that house.

When I got to the hotel, I placed the pack on the bed and headed to the bathroom for a much needed shower. After being in that house, I still could smell the scent of rotten blood on my clothing. Removing my pants and then my boxers, I took a good look at myself in the mirror. Even though my facial features hadn't changed that much since I was a teen, my body had. I was not longer that skinny, shy kid who always managed to get the crap beat out of him.

Turning on the faucet, I splashed cold water on my face and then ran my fingers through my hair, thinking about how fucked up my life was, at least part of it. Stepping away from the sink, I reached into the shower and turned on the water. While I waited for the water to warm, I pulled off my t-shirt. The scar, even though covered with a tattoo, still reminded me every day of the sacrifice I made for my mom. Hidden away beneath it were the words I now and will always live by.

Wrapping a towel around my waist, I sat on the bed next to the backpack I threw on the bed. Staring at it, I contemplated on whether I really wanted to go back to the day I placed the items in it. It held the truth about what really happened to my father so many years ago. Once and for all, I needed to put this shit to rest and move on with my life, but not tonight. Standing, I took the pack and placed it on the small table in the corner. Removing my towel, I slide into bed and turned off the light.

~****~

Dealing with my brother was one thing I couldn't handle today, that and the fact that the sleep I got was next to nil. That damn backpack staring back at me all night long, daring me to pull out the contents, had my mind whirling; that was, until I took hold of it and walked out to my car and threw the damn thing in the trunk. I'm sure the old lady at the office enjoyed my bare ass when I passed her looking at me through the blinds.

As we headed into the attorney's office, I kept

thinking, *"Why the hell would an attorney need to be involved in the affairs of my mom? It wasn't like she had a lot to deal with. She didn't have a lot, and what little she did have was taken by the state to provide for her."*

Taking our seats in the large boardroom, Drew took his place across from where I sat. Looking over to him, I asked, "So what the hell is going on, Drew? Why would we need to involve an attorney? Mom didn't have a whole lot of anything."

"Yeah, well, there is another reason I needed you to come to Stillwater," Drew began. "I haven't been exactly honest with you."

"Spill? What the fuck is going on, Drew?" I asked, getting a little annoyed at his comment.

"A gentleman named Nolan Parks approached me a couple of weeks go. He wants to purchase the land that Mom owned. She left the property to us when we were little. Anyway, they want to build a big fancy mall and office building."

"Really, Drew? Are you that gullible? They'd be lucky to build a single shop on that land, let alone a shopping mall and office building," I advised.

"I'm not talking about the house. That's already gone. I'm talking about the piece of land that was left to her when her parents passed away. I'm talking twenty acres of land, just outside of Stillwater," Drew clarified.

"Are you telling me Mom owned land and she never told us?"

"I don't think she told anyone about it. I don't even think she told Dad about it."

Just as I was about to say something else about it, the attorney we were supposed to be meeting with_walked into the room. He took his place at the head of the table. Before he sat, he addressed us. "Good morning, gentlemen. My name is Everett Lawson. I am the attorney for Nolan Parks and Parks Investments." He held out his hand to Drew and then me. "To make things simple, I will address you both by first name. Shall we get started?"

There was something about this man that I just didn't trust. Then again, there wasn't a lawyer that I did trust. In my opinion they were all shifty bastards who took everything they could get, no matter who it hurt. I may have been a little rude, but there was no way I was going to shake this guy's hand. So instead, I said. "Let's cut the shit, and get on with this."

Looking at me with a surprised look on his face, he replied with a blank look, "Okay, let's." Straightening his already too-perfect tie, he continued as he took his seat. "As you may know, the piece of the land you both own is a prime place for development. Your property is the only piece of land left that hasn't been secured by Parks Investments. We are willing to offer a sizable amount of money for the property."

Looking back over to Drew, I could see that he was getting anxious to find out what the lawyer was about to offer. Taking the lead, I asked. "What is Parks willing to offer?"

"Well, considering the location and the fact that it has been in Parks Investments sights for a long time, I think that twenty million is a fair offer for the property."

I just about lost it. If anything, the property was at most worth thirty thousand. There had to be something else going on with this land that was of such interest to Parks Investments. Unable to swallow the offer, I asked, "Why is our property such an interest to Nolan Parks?"

"Mr Parks has a high stake in the development of that part of Stillwater. The only piece left is the land that you now own," the lawyer replied.

Looking over to Drew, I said, "Come on, bro, we are out of here. If he can't give us a straight answer, then screw him."

"Wait, Jayce, that is a lot of money," Drew said, taking hold of my arm.

"Okay," I said, having an offer of my own. "Here's

the deal. We will accept your twenty million dollar offer, but we also want twenty percent interest in the development of the property. Ten for me and ten for my brother. Take it or leave it."

The look on the attorney's face was a story in itself. I wasn't sure if he thought I was crazy for making such an outrageous offer or if he was actually considering it. Pulling his cell from his pocket, he said, "Excuse me one moment, gentlemen," before he left the room.

As Drew and I sat there, I could see the disbelief in his eyes. He was looking at me like I was fucking crazy for even coming up with such an offer, but when the attorney returned that all changed.

"We will need a little time to draw up the paperwork. Mr. Parks has agreed to your terms. I hope you boys know how wealthy this little transaction is going to make you," he confessed, snapping shut his fancy leather briefcase. "I should have everything ready for you to sign in a couple of days."

CHAPTER SIX

Paige

Somehow I thought that Hawk would be different. He turned out to be like every other guy. The only reason he was acting like a complete gentleman was so he could get in my pants. Just like when I was younger, I gave in to that guy too. You would think that I would have learned by now that the sole purpose for a man to be so nice to a woman was to bury his cock inside her. Pushing from my bed, I knew that I couldn't spend the day wallowing in my regrets. I needed to put my bad choice behind me and get ready for work. I promised Merrill that I would come in a little bit earlier to cover the afternoon crowd. The other bartender wasn't going to be able to come in. Something he had to take care of. Working the extra hours was good for me. Not only did it allow me to make a little extra money, but I also wouldn't be sitting in the small apartment feeling stupid for what happened last night.

Turning on the spray in the shower, I began undressing. It didn't take long before I was under the spray washing away the remaining memories from the night before. Even though the hot water felt good against my skin, I knew that I needed to get going if I was going to make it to the bar on time. Even though Merrill wasn't a stickler for being on time, this was only my third day on the job and I wanted to let him know that he could count on me to be there.

When I arrived at Hell's Gate, there were only a handful of people in the bar, all of which were men. As my eyes adjusted to the darkness of the bar, there was a familiar face sitting at the end of the bar. It was Hawk. The last person that I expected to see. I could have easily walked up to him and slapped him across the face for what he did last night, but I didn't. Instead, I pretended that last night was no more than a one night stand and I didn't give a crap about the way he left so suddenly.

Placing my purse behind the bar, I grabbed one of the black aprons and wrapped it around my waist. Pretending that it didn't matter that he was sitting at the end of the bar watching every move that I made, I made him realize what a mistake he made by leaving the way he did, by flirting with the cute guy sitting a few seats down from him, I knew his eyes were on me the whole time as I leaned over the bar, revealing a little bit of my cleavage as I poured the cute guy another shot of Jack. Even though the guy was cute, the grin he gave me wasn't charming as he took hold of my hand that was holding the bottle of Jack Daniels.

Forcing me to lean in, he pulled on my arm hard enough that I could feel the bruising already taking hold. As I tried to pull away from him, his grip got even tighter as he forced his lips to make contact with mine. Before I knew what happened, he was out of his chair and on the floor. The only thing I could see was Hawk standing over him. He was laying into the guy like he was going to kill him. I must have been yelling at the top of my lungs, because a few moments later, Bucky was on Hawk, pulling him off the poor guy.

"Are you frickin' crazy? You could have killed him," I yelled, standing within inches of his face.

"He shouldn't have forced himself on you the way he did," Hawk replied, trying to pull away from Bucky.

"I could have taken care of myself," I spat back.

"Yeah, I could see that."

He was so infuriating, If I had been a guy, I would have knocked him on his ass. Stepping away, I watched Bucky escort Hawk out of the bar. It was a good thing that Merrill wasn't around, he would have kicked him to the curb and 86'd him. Turning my focus on the cute guy, who was now trying to stand, I walked over to him, hoping he would allow me to help him up.

"You shouldn't have kissed me like that," I said, helping him stand to his feet and to the barstool.

"Yeah, I probably shouldn't have had that last shot

either. Sorry about doing that," he apologized, showing how cute he really was even with a split lip.

"Let me get something for your lip. It looks pretty bad."

"That's okay. I'll be fine. I need to get going anyway. My name is Seth, by the way," he said, turning on the barstool and rising to his feet.

"You take care, Seth," I responded as I watched him slowly make his way to the door.

Once Seth was gone, I went behind the bar and continued with my bar duties. The rest of the night ended up being less exciting. I was surprised, considering the day of the week it was. Hell's Gate had always been busy on Wednesday nights, I'd been told. Just like every other bar, Wednesday was always Ladies Night, and given the number of women that were here, you would think the place would be packed with men just waiting to get lucky. It just didn't make sense that there were two women for every man. Usually it was the other way around, at least according to Bucky.

By the time last call rolled around, I was ready to get out of here and hit the sack. While I was wiping down the bar, Bucky was escorting the last of the drunk customers out the door. When 2:00 a.m. came, everyone was out, all the cleanup was done, and I was out the door. Bucky and I left together, so he offered to make sure I got upstairs to my apartment safely. For being such a big guy, he was a real sweetheart.

~****~

The loud pounding on my door just about sent me through the roof. Rolling over, I took a look at my alarm clock to see that it was only six in the morning. "What the effin hell?" I cursed as I pushed from the bed. Fixing my lopsided messy bun, I headed to the door. There was one bad thing about the apartment, the door had no peep-hole that I could look through to see who was on the other side of the door, only a dark curtain covered the window that had eight individual panes. Staring at the door, instead of pulling back the curtain, I yelled, "Whoever is on the other side, this better be important."

"Don't get your lacy panties in a wad, doll. It's just me, Hawk," he replied from the other side.

Opening the door, there he stood in front of me looking like a model for Starbucks as he held up a crate with two coffees and a brown paper bag with who knew what inside. Taking a coffee from the cardboard crate and the bag filled with goodies, I turned and headed for the small kitchen and took at seat at the small table. I didn't even acknowledge Hawk when he sat right beside me. As much as I was enjoying the vanilla latte and the blueberry muffin, I was still angry at him for not only waking me up so early on my day off, but also because of the way he reacted last night. He had no right to go ballistic the way he did on that poor guy.

"Are you going to talk to me or ignore me while you eat your muffin?" he asked.

"I don't have anything to say to you," I replied, knowing I had plenty to say to him, but preferred to keep my thoughts to myself.

"Well, I have something to say to you," he began. "I shouldn't have attacked that guy the way I did."

"Got that right."

"Who was that guy, anyway? He didn't look like he was your boyfriend or anything."

"He was just a guy who had a little too much to drink. Can we not talk about him? What's done is done."

I had a funny feeling that Hawk wanted to know about the guy rather than talk about something else. Leaving my chair, I picked up my half-eaten muffin and threw it in the garbage. No sooner had I turned around, Hawk was standing right in front of me. All 6'2" of him. The way his body was towering over me made my body tingle all over. And the way his jaw clenched, oh my God, it was the sexiest thing I had ever seen.

I could feel his eyes on me. Even though I was

wearing a t-shirt and shorts, I could feel his eyes burning through the thin material. When I looked down, I could see that not only was my body tingling, but my nipples were at full attention, giving Hawk a perfect view of just how much his presence was turning me on. He moved closer to me. Every step he took caused my heart to beat faster and faster. It didn't even matter that I was mad at him for the way he acted last night. The only thing I could concentrate on was how gorgeous he was and how much I wanted him. I knew, however, that I couldn't give in to him so easily, so for every step he took towards me, I took a step back. I knew I had run out of room the minute my butt hit the handle on the stove.

I could feel the rough yet tender touch of his hand as he placed it on my cheek. There was something different about his touch. Looking up at him. I tried to speak, but nothing would come out. When he lowered his lips to mine, it didn't matter because no words could convey what I felt at that moment. The kiss was tender and the way he pulled me closer made my body pulse with desire. The way I was feeling, you would have thought I was a sex deprived woman. Unable to hold back, I wrapped my arms around him, needing to have his body closer to mine. We were pressed so close together that I could feel the hard peaks of my nipples pressed against the tight muscles of his abs.

His hands slowly moved beneath my t-shirt, sending a wave of electricity to my core. With nothing underneath my shirt, it took him no time at all to find my hard nipples as he gently caressed the tips between his fingers. The touch of his hands on my body left me totally at his mercy. As our kiss deepened, I could feel myself being further possessed by the trance he had over me. It was like my thoughts were not my own as he continued to touch my body the way that he did.

He lifted the thin material of my t-shirt over my head, allowing the cool air of the conditioner to hit the taut peaks of my nipples, making them even harder. His head dipped slightly until his lips touched the curve of my neck, sending even more heat between my legs. The feel of his lips on my body was all I could think about as the pressure between my legs began to build. Unable to stand any longer, he lifted me from the floor, causing my legs to wrap around his muscular waist.

Hawk walked us towards the couch. Before he could set me down, I protested, "Bedroom."

"You got it, doll," he whispered.

I could feel the his shoulders hit the walls of the short hallway as he continued to make his way to my room. It was like he knew exactly where to go. My apartment wasn't very big and there were only two doors for him to choose from. He pushed the partly opened door with his foot and angled our bodies sideways so that he could still hold on to me as he went through the doorway.

As he lowered me to the floor, his soft lips glided over my ear and he softly whispered, "Do you know how bad I want you?"

I knew exactly how he felt, because I wanted him just as bad, if not more. His soft, gentle kisses continued down my neck to the valley between my breasts, where he stopped to take my taut nipple in his mouth. I could feel the swirl of his tongue on the hard peak. My head fell back, taking as much as I could of the pleasure he was giving me. I knew at that point not only were my panties wet, I was pretty sure my shorts were too. Lowering his hands down my body, he slipped his fingers under the waistband and slowly lowered them down my legs.

I knew just by the breath he sucked in, he knew I was soaked with desire for him. Lifting me and placing me gently on the bed, I could hear the beating of my heart as he gently kissed the inside of my right ankle. His kisses continued up my leg, ending at my inner thigh just above my knee. Hawk spread my legs wider as he settled between them. Taking in a deep breath, it finally came. His mouth began consuming me. Gliding his tongue between my folds, he moaned with delight as he lapped and sucked my juices. The fire inside me began to build as he continued his assault on my pussy. In a heated breath, he whispered, "God, I love your pussy, baby."

With those simple words, the fire turned into an inferno, causing me to come with an explosion, sending my body in a freefall spiral. Before I had a chance to breathe, Hawk was pushing his hard cock inside me. Inch by inch, he entered me, filling me with so much pleasure that I couldn't control the orgasm that took hold of my body and erupted. "God, baby, you feel so fucking good. You must have the tightest pussy my cock has ever been inside."

Just like that, another orgasm spilled. That must have been a golden record. Having multiple orgasms wasn't something I thought I would ever be capable of. My body wasn't my own. He had total control over everything I was feeling. Hawk pushed deeper inside me. I could feel my walls grip his length as he thrust harder and faster. It was only after I heard his moans of release that my gates opened once again for him.

CHAPTER SEVEN

Hawk

Laying next to Paige was like being in heaven. Never had a woman made me feel undone as she did. I wasn't sure what was going on with me, but fucking her meant something to me. No longer did I have the urge to turn it into a one time thing. Every other woman I fucked was just that, a good fuck.

Rolling over, I watched Paige sleep. She was the most gorgeous woman I had ever seen. Her body was pure perfection. The sheet had slid just below her ample breasts. I couldn't help but notice how perfect they were. The way they moved with every breath she took. Gorgeous.

Careful not to wake her, I slipped out of bed to grab

my cell from my pants pocket. I knew that it was early morning. Never had I spent the night with a woman after I completely fucked her. Pulling my cell from the pocket of my jeans, I pressed the on button to see that it was only 5:00 in the morning. I really needed to get in touch with Peter to see if he could find anything out about this gorgeous woman.

The security instinct in me kicked into high gear as I made my way to the kitchen where I knew her purse would be. As I tiptoed out of the room, I looked back to the bed to make sure Paige was still sleeping. Making it to the kitchen without waking her, I spotted her purse on the counter. Opening it up, I pulled out her wallet. When I found her driver's license, I took a quick picture and put it back inside. There was something inside one of the small slits. It looked to be a photograph. Pulling it free, I took a look at it. I recognized Paige right away. There were two other people in the photo that may have been her parents. I wasn't sure where it was taken, but it definitely wasn't from here. I could see that there was a mansion or palace of some sort behind them. There was also a body of water behind them. I heard something behind me, so I quickly placed the picture back where I found it, and put her wallet back in her purse. Hearing her footsteps, I hurried to the sink and turned on the faucet. I needed her to think I was getting up for a drink. Cupping my hand under the flow of water, I brought to my mouth and took a drink.

"You know, I do have glasses." I heard her say.

Walking beside me, she reached above her head and pulled out a glass. Holding it out to me, I took it from her and said, "Thanks, doll."

"It's too early for me, I'm going back to bed," she said, taking the glass I filled with water and taking a sip.

"I gotta head out, doll, but I will be back later," I replied.

"Wait. Why do you have to leave? Can't you stay a little longer?" she said.

"Can't, doll. I have a lot of stuff to do. You go back to sleep. I'll even tuck you in." I said with a half smile.

Making sure she was all snuggled in. I kissed her on the forehead and left, making sure to lock the door behind me. As much as I wanted to stay, I needed to leave. Something was going on with me and I wasn't ready to find out what. She was seeping into my head, more than I wanted. I had to think about what I was getting myself into. Soon the kinky stuff would come out. That was one of the reasons I had decided to replace my craving for dominance for one night stands. The last submissive I had, it didn't end well. Matter of fact, it ended very badly. I didn't blame her for leaving me, especially considering my love for dominance nearly killed her.

Pushing back my thoughts, I got in my Mustang to head back to the motel. As I started the engine, I decided to get in touch with Peter. Pulling out my phone, I pulled up my contacts and pressed send.

"Hewitt." I heard him say on the other end.

"Yeah, bro," I replied.

“Hey, Hawk. How are things in Stillwater?” he asked.

“Nothing's changed,” I began. “I need to ask you for a favor. I would do it myself, but I don’t have the resources here.”

“Name it, bro,” Peter replied.

“I need you to check out someone for me. It’s a girl I met out here.”

“Since when are you interested in a girl, other than for a good fuck?”

“Yeah, well, this one is different. There is something about her that has me all undone. You know me, Peter, I’m never interested in just one girl, but this one is making me crazy.”

“What’s her name? I kinda want to know more about this girl myself. See who might finally make you settle down.”

"Her name is Paige Harper. I'm going to send you a copy of her driver's license. Let me know what you find out."

"As soon as I know, you'll know."

"Thanks, Peter. You're the best, bro."

After I finished my call with Peter, I shifted the car into first and backed out of the alley. I could have taken a chance and parked it out front, but I didn't want that burly son-of-a bitch from Hell's Gate to see my car and wonder if I was around making more trouble.

Before I headed back to the motel, there was one place that I needed to go. It was the one place where I could think and clear my head.

~****~

Pulling up to Boomer Lake brought back so many memories. Even in my younger days, I remember riding the nine miles on my bike just to get away and think about stuff. Mostly just to get away from the shit storm at home. Following the road around the large lake, I finally came upon my favorite spot. Putting the car in first and setting the brake, I got out and began my walk to the shore where my thinking rock, as I called it, was. I used to always perch on it while either fishing or just trying to get rocks to skip along the glassy surface of the water. Never mastered either one of them.

Looking out across the water, I took my place on my favorite spot and began thinking about everything. It didn't matter what I thought about, my mind always drifted back to Paige. The more I thought about her, the more I knew there was so much more to her than there appeared. She wasn't the hometown girl that she was portraying. Remembering how she looked in the photo, I almost wished I had the time to take a picture of it as well. There was something about that photo that didn't fit. Was she on some sort of vacation with her family? If she was, why were she and the other two people dressed so regally? It didn't make sense. As I wondered about these things, I also remembered the feisty side of her when we first bumped into each other. It was that side of her that had me wanting to know more about her. Who would have thought that we would have ended up in the same shit of a town? Her being here had made my trip more bearable.

Pushing from the large rock, I headed back to my car. It was just past 6:00 a.m., and I needed a shower and to get together with my brother to go over this shit with my mom. Hopefully everything was almost done with that. I knew that Drew was working on the funeral arrangements. Mom didn't have many friends in Stillwater, my dad made sure of that. The relatives she did have were so far way that it made no sense to ask them to come even though Drew insisted on letting them know. Half of them I didn't even know.

Parking the Mustang, my cell began to chime. Pulling it from my pants pocket, it was Peter.

"Hey, bro," I said.

"Hey, don't get too excited," Peter paused as he took in a breath, "Your little girlfriend has no history. It's like she didn't exist up until twelve months ago. It's really strange, Hawk. I'm going to do some more digging, maybe we can figure her out."

"Whatever you come up with, let me know. I want, no, I need to know everything about her."

As I hung up, I tried to think of why a person would only be on record for twelve months. The only thing I could come up with was they were hiding something or didn't want to be found. It just didn't make sense with Paige. What the hell was she hiding?

When I got back to the motel, I stripped off my clothes and turned the water to the shower on and waited for it to warm up. Looking in the mirror, I saw something I hadn't seen before. A man unable to find himself and what he really wanted in life. My life up until a few weeks ago wasn't complicated. I did as I wanted with no regrets. Now, it seemed my past was finally catching up to me. I regretted the many women I had fucked and how I may have broken their hearts. Being called an asshole on numerous occasions seemed like a compliment now that I looked back at what I did to them. I was a damn dickhead.

Finishing my shower, I grabbed my cell and called Drew. I needed to find out how this funeral was going to play out. Mom didn't have anything when she died, so the expense of the funeral was on Drew and me. I suggested that we just get her cremated, but Drew won out and now she will be buried six feet under.

"Hey, Drew, just called to see what your plans were for the day. We need to discuss the arrangement for Ma's funeral," I said.

"Everything has been taken care of. All you need to do is show up on Friday," Drew advised.

"Okay, I'll be there," I replied.

Before I hung up I heard Drew on the other end. "Jayce."

"Yeah," I replied.

"Nolan Parks' attorney called. The funds from the sale of the land should be wired to our bank accounts by tomorrow. Just thought I'd let you know."

"Thanks for the info," I said, finishing the call.

At least one good thing came out of this. Drew and I would be set for life. *"Thanks, Mom,"* I said to myself as I slipped my phone back in my pocket. Snatching my keys from the nightstand, I headed out to grab something to eat. I knew that it was Paige's day off and I wanted to do nothing more than to spend the day with her. Just then, I came up with the idea of taking her to Boomer Lake for a little picnic. Hopefully, I could get her to open up to me about who she really was.

CHAPTER EIGHT

Paige

After Hawk left, I couldn't go back to sleep. The only thing I could think about was him and how good it felt with him beside me. I loved the way he wrapped his arms around me and held me close. Looking up at the ceiling for the last half-hour, I finally decided to nix the sleeping in and headed to the kitchen to make some coffee. As I prepared the coffee, I thought about what I could do today. It was my first day off since I moved down here a week ago. I wasn't even sure what there was to do in this small town. While I waited for the coffee to brew, I Googled Stillwater, OK, on my phone and waited while it searched my request. Not a whole lot going on here, that was for sure. Even though moving here was the safest bet for me, at least to keep a low profile and off the radar of my uncle, I missed the excitement of New York. There was always something to do on any given day.

Lost in my thoughts, I heard the beeping of the coffee maker letting me know that the coffee was ready. As I poured a cup, I thought about Hawk and what he was doing at this very moment. I knew he said he would be back later, I just didn't know how much later. Setting my phone on the counter, I decided to take a little trip to the market down the street. Reaching for my purse, I wanted to see if I had enough cash or if I needed to get some from my secret stash that I had neatly tucked away in my sock drawer. It was the safest place I could think of. I couldn't risk opening up a checking account again and my uncle finding me. That was one of the mistakes I made in New York. I should have never listened to my friend Nikki back in New York. She was one of those types that didn't trust anyone. I remember the first time I went to her apartment, she had so many locks on her door, I prayed we wouldn't have to leave in a hurry. But that wasn't the worst of it. The grates on her windows made me think that something else was going on with her aside from wanting to feel safe.

Pulling my purse from the counter, I reached inside for my wallet. As I pulled it out, it occurred to me that it wasn't snapped shut. I found this to be odd since I always made sure that it was. Opening it up, I looked inside, mostly to make sure the one thing I kept hidden inside was still there. Again, something was odd. It was the way the picture was placed in the hidden compartment of my wallet. The picture was face up as I pulled it out. I would have never put in back that way. I always placed it face down. Thinking that I might have been in a hurry or something, I continued to pull it out. Looking at the picture, I remembered the day that it was taken. It was the day a formal announcement was made to the people of Kierabali of the man that was chosen for me to marry. To this day, I still haven't ever met the man I was supposed to marry.

Chucking the weirdness of my wallet mishap to my forgetfulness, I took my brimming hot coffee mug to the bathroom and began getting ready for the day. It was still early and I wasn't sure when Hawk would be showing up on my doorstep. I never gave him my cell number, so it wouldn't surprise me if he just showed up. Stripping off my t-shirt and panties, I stepped in the shower, but not before I placed my iPod in the docking station. As Train radiated off the walls, my body swayed to the beat.

The spray of the hot water felt so good against my skin. I would have loved to have taken a bath instead, but there was no time. Back home in Kierabali, I had a jetted tub in my room. Every chance I got, I would soak inside the tub and think about how much I wanted my life to change. The day finally came when I decided to leave the small island and come to the States. The land of opportunity. It was the scariest thing I had ever done, but I knew that if I was ever going to be able to control my own destiny, I needed to break free. I knew my parents would have wanted me to be happy. Even though the marriage thing was pre-arranged, they knew how unhappy I was. It was something they couldn't stop even if they wanted to. And now with my uncle in charge, he would stop at nothing to make sure it did happen.

As I finished drying my hair, I heard a knock at the door. I had only been in the bathroom for a little while and I knew that it couldn't be Hawk. Placing my hair blower on the counter I headed to the front door. When I opened the door, I was surprised to see that Merrill was standing with Nikki. I couldn't believe she was here. Pulling her in for a hug, I said, "God, I've missed you."

"I've, missed you too. We need to talk," Nikki said, pulling away from our embrace.

"I'll leave you two to catch up," Merrill said, heading back down to the bar.

I held the door open and allowed her to walk through. I could tell by the expression on her face, she wasn't too happy with my current living situation. Closing the door, I said, "It's not the ideal home, but for now it works.

"Turning to face me, she said, "What kind of trouble are you in, Paige?"

"What do you mean?" I replied.

"Two men stopped by the coffee shop asking about you. They wanted to know if I knew where you may have gone," she said, plopping down on the couch.

"What did you tell them, Nikki?" I asked with concern.

"I told them that I didn't know and that you left no forwarding address. I figured it was none of their business."

Opening the door, I looked down the steps and as far as I could down the alley. The only thing I could think about was, *"What if someone followed her here from New York?"* I had a pretty good idea who was asking about me. It had to be some of my uncle's men. Seeing that there was no one around, I closed the door and walked over to where Nikki was sitting. Even though she was my best friend, this was something that I couldn't share with her. The last thing I wanted was for her to be involved in my problems, and also what would happen if they ever found out that she knew where I was.

Sitting beside her, I pulled her in for another hug. "I'm so glad you're here, Nikki." I didn't know what to tell her about my situation, but I knew that I needed to make up something fast. Looking over at the small end table, I saw a magazine that I purchased because of the front cover and the story that was tied to it. It was then that my cover-up began. “I had to get away from New York because of who my father was. He owed some people a lot of money and they have been looking for him for a long time. They think I may know where he is. This may be why they came to the coffee shop looking for me.”

“Oh God, Paige. Are you in danger?” Nikki questioned, looking in my eyes for answers.

“It’s not me that they want, at least I don’t think so,” I answered.

“What if they want to hold you for ransom or something? You see it in the movies all the time. Girl gets kidnapped in exchange for payment.” Nikki said.

“Nikki, come on. Now you are being too paranoid.”

“Just saying, Paige,” she argued.

~****~

It was getting close to noon, and I still hadn't heard from Hawk. I didn't want to wait around the apartment for him, so Nikki and I decided to check out the town. There wasn't really that much to see. It would probably take all of an hour to see the sights. Locking my door, we headed down the steps only to be greeted by a gorgeous man dressed in dark jeans and a gray t-shirt. Looking over to Nikki, I could tell she was goggling over Hawk. Nudging her side, I brought her back to reality as I introduced them. "I didn't know when you would be coming back, so we decided to check out the town. This is Nikki. Nikki, this is Hawk."

Hawk extended his hand and said,"Nice to meet yah."

Nikki just stood there unable to speak. As she was still holding onto his hand, Hawk smiled. "I'm gonna need that hand back, doll."

I could see the red on Nikki's cheeks as she quickly

pulled her hand away. "Sorry."

"Not a problem," Hawk said. "I wanted to know if Paige wanted to go to the lake and have a picnic, but since you're here, I'd like to extend the invitation. If that's okay with you, Paige."

"That sounds great. I'm sure Nikki doesn't have any immediate plans, " I replied.

"Good, it's settled," Hawk announced.

Hawk led the way as we followed behind. Nikki was slobbering more than I was at the sight of his tight ass. It was going to be fun seeing what was going to happen at the lake with her. Nikki was gorgeous. It surprised me that she was working at a coffee shop instead of modeling. Even though she was gorgeous and could have her pick of any man she wanted, she was very shy when it came to them. It was like she got tongue-tied whenever she was around them, almost intimidated by them. This was why it didn't bother me that she goggled over Hawk the way she did. I knew she wouldn't do anything other than take in his oh-so-handsome features.

Hawk pulled up to the lake about fifteen minutes later. The view of the lake from the car was spectacular. I couldn't wait to get out and take in the full view. Once we were completely stopped, I swung open my door and flipped the seat forward so Nikki could get out. The air out here was much different than the air in town. It was so crisp. It reminded me of back home, where the palace was close to the ocean. That was about the only thing I missed about Kierabali.

I stepped up to the water and took a seat on a large rock while looking out over the water. In the distance I could see a couple of people in a small boat who looked to be fishing. Everything about this little town was so different than the big city. There was no rush. People seemed more relaxed. I turned my body to see that Hawk was already busy spreading out a blanket on a grassy area while Nikki went to grab some more things from Hawk's car. Pushing off of the rock, I went to where Nikki was to see if I could offer her any help. It was then that I noticed a black SUV parked off the road about 50 yards away. My heart began pounding so hard, I thought I was going to pass out. The only thing I could think of was to try and make an excuse to leave. I had a funny feeling that whoever was in the SUV was not there to enjoy the scenery.

CHAPTER NINE

Paige

The minute Nikki looked over at me, she knew something was wrong. Angling her body my way, she looked over to where my eyes were and saw the black SUV. With a slight nod of her head, she asked, "Friends of yours?"

"I think I might be in trouble, Nikki. I need to get out of here without Hawk getting suspicious," I replied.

"So you need an excuse or something."

"Yeah."

"I will only do this for you, but you have to tell me

what is really going on with you, Paige."

"I will tell you everything, but for now I really need to get out of here," I began pleading as the SUV began to move up the road towards where we were.

"Okay, here goes nothing." Nikki said, before she contorted her body in such a way that it looked like she had popped her shoulder out of place.

With a small wink she screamed, "Holy fucking crumb cakes!"

Playing along, I said, "Oh my God, Nikki, are you okay?"

I said it just loud enough that it got Hawk's attention. Dropping everything he had in his hand, he quickly jogged over to where we were standing. I was glad that the trunk door was still open, hiding what really went on with Nikki's shoulder. Hawk was beside us in a split second trying to figure out what was happening. The minute he looked at Nikki, he could see that she was hurt.

This was my cue. "Hawk we need to leave. Nikki needs to see a doctor."

"Tell me what happened?" Hawk asked.

Looking to Nikki, I waited to see what story she was going to conjure up. "I tripped over my damn shoelace and fell against the roof of the car. Damn that hurts," she hissed, holding her shoulder while showing a look of excruciating pain on her face.

Hawk believed her little act. She should be nominated for an Academy award for her performance. I tried not to laugh as Hawk helped her to the front seat by making sure that she didn't do further damage to her shoulder. I watched as Hawk rounded the front of the car while I finished gathering the picnic items that he had laid out. The trunk was still open, so it didn't take me very long to throw everything inside and get in the car behind the driver's seat. Taking a quick look over my shoulder, I could still see the SUV coming towards us. With a quick breath, I said with panic, "You better hurry, Hawk. I think Nikki is going to pass out."

I was thankful that she saw my fear and began acting like she actually was going to pass out. I could feel Hawk increase the speed of the Mustang as he stepped harder on the gas pedal, passing the SUV. I didn't get a good look at who was inside, but whoever was in the SUV must have sensed something, because they came to a complete stop, throwing dirt behind them. As we got further away from them, I noticed that they weren't moving. It was like time stood still. It didn't make sense that they wouldn't be following us.

Turning my focus to the front of the car, Hawk's gorgeous eyes were staring back at me through the rearview mirror. I wondered how long he had been staring at me. My question was answered when he said, "You've been looking back at that black SUV since we left. Somebody you know?"

At that moment, my heart sank into my stomach. Thank God for Nikki: once again, she saved the day. " Hawk, can you pull over for a second? I think I'm going to be sick."

Hawk immediately cranked the wheel and pulled the car over to the side of the road. Before Nikki had a chance to open her door, Hawk was right there to assist her. This was my chance, I took another quick look over my shoulder, just to make sure the SUV hadn't moved. When I couldn't see it parked the last time I looked back, I began to scan the area to see if I could see it. It was nowhere, at least not where I could see it. Once again, my heart fell to my stomach. It was then I realized there was nothing I could do, no matter how hard I tried to avoid what I knew, in the back of my mind, was going to happen, I took a deep breath, calmed myself, and decided to let whatever was going to be, be.

Closing my eyes and praying for the best, I heard Hawk get back in the driver's seat and pull away from the side of the road. Maybe I had been anxious for no reason. When I left New York, I was very careful not to leave anything behind that pointed to where I was going. The only person who knew anything was Nikki, and I trusted her with my life.

~****~

When we got to the hospital, Nicki was checked in and taken back to one of the ER rooms. I was glad that they weren't very busy and she was helped right away. One thing I wasn't glad about was Hawk and I were left alone in the waiting area. Taking our seat beside each other, I knew by the way his jaw was clenched, he wanted answers. There was no way I was going to say anything. The longer we sat in silence, the longer it gave me time to think about what I was going to say to him.

"You need to tell me why you were so interested in that black SUV out at the lake. I find it pretty strange that an expensive vehicle like that would be there in the first place," he grilled.

"You know what, Hawk, I was thinking the same thing. I was watching it to see where they were going," I tried to say convincingly.

"Somehow, that doesn't sound very convincing. No

matter, I got the plate number when we passed them. I'll have one of the guys run it for me," Hawk advised.

"One of the guys?" I questioned.

"Yeah, from Jagged Edge Security," he began. "I work there."

"Crap, crap, crap," I thought to myself. If he finds out who the vehicle belongs to then he will know who I really am. Shrugging my shoulders, I tried to act cool. "Doesn't matter. Who cares, anyway?"

Before Hawk could comment, a nurse came through the ER doors with Nikki walking right beside her. The way she looked was as if nothing had ever happened. Walking up to her, I gave her a light squeeze, letting her know how much I appreciated what she did.

"She's all set. The doctor just popped her shoulder back into place," the nurse advised.

I waited for Nikki to sign the necessary documents

while Hawk went to go get the car. I knew I had some explaining to do the minute we got back to my apartment. I just wasn't sure how much information I was actually going to share with her. I knew I was going to need to do some explaining on why I lied to her in the first place.

As we walked outside the hospital, Hawk was already waiting for us. His tall, muscular frame was leaning against the fender of his Mustang while his cell was to his ear. I had no clue as to whom he was talking with, but I found it a little strange when he ended the call as soon as he saw us. Pushing from the car, he opened the passenger side door and waited for us to get in. I could tell by the look on his face that he wasn't very happy. Before I slipped into the passenger seat, I looked at him and asked, "Is everything okay?"

Leaning in, he kissed me on the forehead and said softly, "We need to talk."

Even knowing that I was finally caught, just the sound of his voice next to my ear made my heart sing and my panties wet. Looking into his eyes, I tried to see if there was something behind them that would tell me if he was concerned or angry. When he brushed his hand along my cheek and said," Buckle up," I knew it was definitely concern on his face.

Taking hold of the seatbelt, I draped it over my shoulder and snapped it into place. Nothing more was said as Hawk pulled away from the front of the hospital. Looking out the window, I kept wondering what was going to happen when we got to my apartment. All I could think about was the interrogation I was going to get.

It wasn't long until we were there. My mind was reeling a mile a minute. Hawk turned down the alley on the side of the Hell's Gate bar. Stopping just in front of my apartment, he looked over to me and said, "I need to take care of a few things, then I am coming back and we are going to talk."

"About what?" I asked, trying to play dumb.

"About what you are hiding from me," he replied.

"I don't know what you're talking about, Hawk. I have nothing to hide from you."

"We'll see. I'll be back."

Hawk leaned over and gave me a kiss on the lips, which just about had me leaping over the console to take him right there. If it wasn't for Nikki in the backseat, I would have done just that. Opening the door, I pushed the seat forward and waited for Nikki to get out. I watched Hawk drive away, still feeling the slight tingle from his kiss on my lips. Nikki grabbed my arm to get my attention before she pulled me to the steps to my apartment.

"Come on, Lucy, you have some 'splaining to do," Nikki hinted.

I knew all too well I had some explaining to do. I just didn't know where to start. I just hoped that I was making the right decision to tell Nikki the truth.

~****~

"So that's the whole story. I'm sorry I lied to you about my dad and all that," I said.

"So let me get this straight. You are a princess from some island in the South Pacific, and you ran away from there because you were suppose to marry some guy you have never met, and now you think your uncle, who has basically everything to gain, is here to find you and take you back," Nikki explained.

"Yep, that's about right," I said. "I'm begging you, Nikki, please don't tell anyone my secret. You have to promise."

"Pinky swear," Nikki said, holding up her hand with her small finger sticking straight up.

Entwining our fingers together, we shook on it. Leaning over to me, Nikki gave me the biggest hug and said softly, "You are my friend, Paige, Princess Isabelle Moraco of Kierabali, I will take your secret to the grave with me. What if Hawk finds out who owns that SUV?"

"I don't know. I guess I will just have to wait and see what he actually finds out before I decide on what to tell him. I'm afraid the more people who know about me, the more I will be putting them at risk. My uncle will stop at nothing to get me back to Kierabali. I think he would even have someone killed if they got in his way."

"Oh my God, Paige, you told me everything. Am I in danger?" Nikki asked with fear in her eyes.

"I don't think so. Unless you tell someone. Then I might have to strangle you," I said, trying to act serious.

"That is not funny, Paige."

The more I thought about what Nikki said, the more I regretted my decision to tell her the truth. I knew my uncle all too well. He was a ruthless man. His only concern was having the power to rule over Kierabali. It didn't matter how many people he had to hurt to get whatever he wanted. He was capable of anything.

CHAPTER TEN
Hawk

After dropping off Paige, I went back to the motel to see if there was any more information on her. I wanted to make sure my full attention was on the information that Peter found out for me regarding black SUV that suddenly showed up at the lake. It was definitely not a vehicle you would find in Stillwater.

When I got to my room, I noticed that the door wasn't locked. I knew there was no way in hell that I would have left the door unlocked. Going to the trunk, I opened it and pulled my Magnum from the hidden compartment I had built on the the side. I was pretty sure that whoever broke into my room was more than likely already gone, but there was no way I was going to take that chance.

Slowly pushing open the door, I held my gun up. As I peeked around the corner, I could see whoever got inside did a number on the room. Everything was torn apart. The things in my duffel bag were scattered on the floor. Every drawer was pulled open or laying face down next to my things. Even the mattress to the bed was flipped over. I had no idea what the hell was going on, but I had a pretty good idea it had to do with the SUV at the lake. Placing my Magnum between my waistband and the small of my back, I pulled out my cell and called Peter.

"I hope you have some info for me bro. My motel room has been ransacked," I cursed.

"Yeah. You're not going to like what we found out. That SUV is registered to some international diplomat," Peter began. "What would an international diplomat be doing in Stillwater, Hawk?"

"I don't know, but I am going to find out. There is something strange about this whole thing. I think it has something to do with Nikki, Paige's friend. The SUV showing up just after Nikki came to town is a little too coincidental. And the fact that Nikki got hurt or at least seemed to be hurt is starting to make sense. I think she wanted to get as far away as possible from that SUV. I'm going to be having a little chat with Paige. In the meantime, maybe it wouldn't hurt to do a little search on Nikki as well," I suggested.

"Do you know Nikki's last name?" Peter asked.

"No, I don't know anything about her, other than Paige and her were friends back in New York."

"I'll see what I can find out. I'll get back to you as soon as I come up with anything."

The minute I hung up with Peter, I started thinking about the kind of trouble Nikki could be in. I remembered that Sabrina had a friend named Nikki. Agnew it was a long shot, but it would be worth it to find out if she was the same one. Swiping the screen, I searched for Cop's number.

"Hey Cop, its Hawk. I have a question for you," I said

"Shoot bro," Cop replied.

"Didn't Sabrina have a friend named Nikki?" I asked.

"Yeah, they worked together at the Happy Cow. Nikki Jennings, why?" Cop asked.

"Because I think she is in Stillwater. I think she may be in some sort of trouble. An SUV showed up at Boomer Lake. It stuck out like a sore thumb, so I got the plate number and had Peter run it. Thought it was kinda strange that it showed up after Nikki did."

"What does she look like?" Cop asked.

"Well, she is gorgeous, but not in the same way that Paige is. Nikki has that model look to her. You know, tall, thin, nice body, the kind you see on the cover of one of those girly magazines."

"Yep, I know exactly. The girl you just described sounds just like her. I'll check with Brie to be certain. She would know if Nikki was making any traveling plans."

After I hung up, I felt better knowing that Paige's, Nikki, might be Sabrina's, Nikki, as well. I just needed to find out what the deal was with her, and what kind of trouble she was in. I told Paige that I would be back to talk with her and knowing what I do, it needed to be alone. I just needed to come up with an excuse to break away from Nikki.

~****~

I must have sat on the lumpy bed in my motel room for at least two hours before I decided to wait until tomorrow to have that chat with Paige. After explaining that I wouldn't be able to make it back for our little chat, I got the feeling that she was relieved that our little talk wouldn't be happening until tomorrow. Postponing the chat gave me some time to think about my next move. Even though I didn't have a laptop or a tablet, I still had my smartphone. Pulling up the internet, I began searching anything that had to do with Paige Harper. Usually something would come up,but there was nothing. Paige didn't even have a Facebook page. I found this to be odd, especially since the majority of all the people in the US had one.

With no results for Paige, I decided to try Nikki Jennings instead. The web lit up with her name. Not only did she have a Facebook page, but she also showed having a Twitter account and several other accounts. Clicking on her Facebook link. I opened her page. *"Wow, this girl was very popular with 3094 Facebook friends. Who the hell has that many friends?"* I thought to myself. Scrolling down her timeline, I tried out find anything that would tell me who she was and who her friends were. When nothing stuck out, I began looking at her friends list. Maybe someone would stand out there. As I began scrolling down her friends list, I noticed that Paige wasn't one of her friends. I found this odd, considering she came down all the way from New York to visit her. Another thing I thought was odd, was that Sabrina wasn't amongst her friends list either.

Looking at the time on my phone, I realized that I hadn't had anything to eat since this morning. That would explain why my stomach was talking to me. Pushing from the bed, I grabbed my keys from the nightstand and decided to head over for a bite at the corner diner. It was the best place to eat in this town, unless of course you wanted a hamburger and fries. As I got in the car and began backing up, I noticed the same SUV parked across the street at the town park. The fact that it was parked next to a weeping willow tree didn't do much to hide their presence. Because I was in one of those moods, I decided to go check it out and find out what it was that they wanted and why the fuck they were following me.

Stepping on the gas, I headed their way. They must have seen me approaching, because not sooner I punched the gas, they were pulling away from the curb. There was no way I was going to let them get away this time. As they sped up, so did I. I knew I was breaking every speed limit posted, but since they had a head start on me, I had to increase in my speed if I was going to catch up with them. Turning the corner, I could hear the wheels of the SUV squeal. If I had to guess, I would say they took that corner at 40 MPH. It was a good thing I was in my Mustang because turning the corner with my car was no problem at that speed.

I was gaining on them when a beat-up station wagon pulled out in front of me. Trying to avoid crashing into it, I yanked my wheel to the right which caused my car to hit the curb and jump up onto the sidewalk missing the little flower shop. Looking back in my rearview mirror, I could see the back of the SUV as it drove away. There was no way I would be able to catch them now. Slamming my hands down on my steering wheel, I was beaten once again and left empty. Contemplating my next move, there was a light tap on my window. Looking over, I saw a little old lady wearing wire framed glasses that reminded me of Mrs. Beasley standing outside. Rolling down the window I heard her say, "You should be a little bit more careful, I almost hit this beautiful car."

"Yes, ma'am. Just in a bit of a hurry. I'll try to be more careful," I replied, feeling guilty at the way she was looking a me.

Patting me on the shoulder, I watched as she turned away and got back inside her beat-up station wagon that looked to be just about as old as her. Putting my car in reverse, I slowly backed off of the curb and headed down the street to my original destination.

Parking the Mustang in front of the diner, I got out and noticed an attractive girl holding the hand of a little boy. I assumed that by the resemblance that the little boy was her son. It wasn't until she turned around that I recognized that face. It was Erica, the girl I use to get my kicks with whenever I was on leave to see my brother. I knew the minute she looked up at me, she knew exactly who I was. There wasn't anything that I wanted to say to her, so when she started towards me, I was at a loss for words. The closer she got, the more I could feel my chest tighten. Even though everything we did together was consensual, some of the stuff was pretty hardcore, even for me. She claimed that she loved everything I did to her. I felt guilty as hell when the bruises and red marked began showing up the next day when we were at it again.

"Jayce, is that you?" she asked softly.

"Hey Erica, how are you?" I replied, shoving my hands in my pockets.

"Good. Wow, you look different," she answered.

Looking down at the small hand in hers, I followed it to the little face that was staring up at me. Taking in the little guy's features, I could see that there was something about him that was all too familiar. His eyes. It was like looking back at myself twenty-seven years ago. Kneeling down in front of him, I looked up at Erica and asked, "Who's this little guy?"

"This is my son. His name is Charlie," Erica said.

"Well, hello Charlie. My name is Hawk. At least that is what everyone calls me," I said, holding out my hand.

I just about fell over when he took hold of my hand and said very softly. "Nice to meet you, sir. Did you know I have a red truck?"

Letting go of my hand, he reached behind him and pulled a little red Tonka truck from his back pocket. "Wow, that's a really nice truck," I said with a smile.

"We are meeting Mom and Dad for dinner. It was really nice seeing you Jayce," Erica said.

Standing to my feet, I watched as the two of them headed for the steps of the diner. Knowing they would be inside, I turned the other way and headed back to my car. A hamburger and fries sounded better.

CHAPTER ELEVEN

Paige

Hearing that Hawk wasn't coming back to my apartment was the best news I could have had. It meant that I had one more day to come up with an explanation for what happened today. I had a pretty good feeling that the little act Nikki put on wasn't as convincing as it looked. I thought maybe Nikki could give me a few pointers on how to make up a story that would sound believable enough even for Hawk.

After telling Nikki my pathetic story we decided to chill on the couch, Nikki ended up ordering pizza while I opened a bottle of wine that I took from the bar. Merrill was really good about the employees taking liquor from the bar. He didn't really care as long as there was money in the till to cover the charge, and what I meant by charge was the fifteen percent mark-up he had on all of his liquor.

Pouring a glass for myself and Nikki, I shifted my feet in her direction and held out a half-full glass to her. Taking a seat beside her, we sat in silence for a minute enjoying the peace and quiet. At least until she asked, “So what are you going to tell the hot alpha-male?”

“I’m not going to say anything, and you better not either,” I replied.

“I pinky swore with you. That is like the holiest of all swears,” Nikki confirmed, placing her hand across her heart.

“I know you did. I just need to come up with something that Hawk will believe,” I hinted.

“Why don't you just play dumb and tell him you don't know anything?” Nikki suggested.

After Nikki told me what I should do, maybe she

was right. If I played dumb, at least I wouldn't have to remember any details of the story I would be telling him. I knew how lies could snowball into more lies and then even more lies. Drinking the last of my wine, I heard a light knock on the door. It had to be the pizza delivery guy. Walking over to the door. I pulled back the dark curtain and looked out. Holding a white box with the lettering 'Santino's' across the top in big red letters, it was definitely the pizza delivery guy. Giving him the correct amount and a healthy tip, I took the box and closed the door. Nikki was already in the kitchen getting some plates and refilling our glasses with wine. It was nice having her here. I didn't have very many friends, given my current situation, but I knew that my secret was safe with her.

After we polished off the bottle of wine and consumed all but two pieces of the 'everything under the sun' pizza, Nikki suggested we go to Hell's Gate for a game of pool and a drink. I wasn't that keen on playing pool, so I suggested we go for a quick drink and relax. Grabbing her things, we headed down the stairs to the back entrance of the bar. The minute we opened the door, we could hear the music and the faint sound of male and female conversations taking place. Merrill was behind the bar talking with an attractive young girl sitting on the other side. Although I would have preferred to sit at a table, Nikki convinced me that we needed to be at the bar between two cute guys. As hopping as the place was, I was surprised to find that there were two empty seats available at the bar, and being between two hot guys was an added bonus, at least for Nikki.

As we took our seats, Merrill spotted us and came over to take our order. Nikki ordered some tooty-fruity drink that I had never heard of and I ordered a Cosmopolitan. Right when Merrill stepped away, the guy sitting next to Nikki began to hit on her. I couldn't hear everything he was saying, but whatever it was brought a smile to her face. It wasn't long after we got our drinks that Nikki and the guy got up and headed to the pool tables. Spinning my chair, I took my drink and followed them over to where the tables were set up. I would have never thought of Nikki as the kind of girl who would even be interested in playing pool.

After I sat watching them for a while, another guy

came over and sat down at a table just inches away from me. Not wanting to seem like I was checking him out. I picked up my drink and took a sip. Getting a pretty good look at him, he was very good looking. His hair was light brown and his eyes were a lighter color. Considering how dark the bar was, I was pretty sure they were either blue or green. When he got up and placed four quarters on the table, my eyes were focused on the nicest ass I had ever seen. Hawk was gorgeous in every aspect of the word, but this guy wasn't too bad either.

Drawing my attention away from his ass, I was greeted with a smile that made me so embarrassed, I knew for certain that he knew exactly what I was looking at. Watching him walk back to his table, I turned my head in the opposite direction so that I could hide the redness that was burning like fire on my cheeks. Thinking I was pretty safe, I heard the screech of the chair against the wood floor. Turning toward the sound, there he was pulling the chair out that was positioned right across from me. As I looked at him, he was even more handsome than he looked from a distance.

Setting his drink on the table, he asked with a slight whisper, "Do you mind if I join you?"

I knew that my mouth must have been hanging open long enough for him to realize that I was gawking at him. With an embarrassed breath, I replied, "Yeah." I was thankful that I was at least able to get that much out.

"You look very familiar to me. Have we met before?" he asked.

"I don't think so. I have only been in town for a week or so. I'm Paige, by the way." I said as I held out my hand.

Expecting him to just shake it like a normal person, he lowered his head and lightly placed a kiss on the back of my hand. As he looked back up at me, he said, "My name is Victor Walsh."

"Well, it is nice to meet you, Mr. Walsh," I said.

"Please call me Victor," he demanded.

"Okay, Nice to meet you, Victor," I said with a smile.

As we began talking there was yelling coming from the two guys that were playing at the next table over from where Nikki and her guy friend were. I thought for sure something bad was going to happen the way they were slinging profanities back and forth. As I watched the two guys argue, one of them finally gave up by planting his fist against the other guy's cheek. I couldn't believe what I was seeing. Nikki's pool partner looked over and all of a sudden he was part of the fight.

This was the most excitement I had seen in a long time. I wasn't sure what all the drama was about, but I knew one thing for sure, there was way too much testosterone in this place for me. Rising to my feet. I headed over to where Nikki was. By the look on her face, I could tell that she was just as amazed as I was. It wasn't until Victor stepped in that I realized the little argument at the pool table between two guys ended up being a brawl with four guys going at it. All I knew was that we really needed to get out of there and fast. Grabbing Nikki by the arm, I pulled her towards me and said, "Let's get out of here, before things get really bad."

Taking my lead, Nikki followed behind me to the back of the bar where I knew we would be safe, away from the male egos. With our drinks in hand, we slipped inside Merrill's office and shut the door. Even with the door closed, I could still hear the commotion outside. I wasn't sure what was going on, but it sounded like every male in the bar was getting in on the action.

Sitting on the plush couch that had to have been from the seventies, Nikki and I looked at each other and tapped our glasses together, with Nikki saying, "Here's to men and all their bullshit hormones."

I had to laugh at her toast. Not because it was funny, but because she was so spot on. As we sat there perfectly content to be away from all the drama, the door to the office opened. Thinking that the only person it could be was Merrill, we were both surprised to see Victor opening the door.

"It is like a damn zoo out there. Mind if I join your solitude?"

Nikki and I just looked at each other and began to laugh. Who says stuff like that anyway? After we had finally composed ourselves, I said, "Sure, the more the merrier."

There wasn't any other place to sit except behind Merrill's desk. Victor took a seat like he belonged there. It was kind of strange seeing him sitting behind the large desk. There was something very commanding about him sitting there. Like he belonged there.

"So, crazy stuff out there," he said.

"Yeah. What were they fighting about anyway?" I asked.

"I'm not sure, I think it may have had something to do with a girl," he assumed.

There was no way that the two guys playing pool

were fighting about a girl. If I had to guess it was more about cheating. Finishing the last of my drink, I had enough excitement for one night, Pushing to my feet, I looked over to Nikki and said, "I don't know about you, but I think I am ready to call it a night. Before she could respond, Victor was standing.

"Wait, I haven't even had the chance to buy you a drink," he offered.

"There's no need, really. I'm good," I replied.

Nikki and I were at the door when Victor asked, "Can I at least ask you to join me for dinner?"

"It's late and I am really not hungry, but thanks for the offer. Maybe another time," I suggested.

The last thing I needed was another male to deal with. Hawk was enough for me. As cute as Victor was, there wasn't anything that could convince me to have dinner with him.

By the time we made it to the apartment it was

midnight. After we left Merrill's office, Merrill began quizzing us about what had happened at the pool tables. There really wasn't anything that I could tell him, other than my opinion on the whole matter. One thing I did tell him was that testosterone and liquor didn't mix.

~****~

Saying our good nights, Nikki made herself as comfortable as possible on the couch, while I went to my bedroom. Slipping under the covers, I was beginning to think about the guy at the bar. Then I began to think about Hawk. I couldn't believe I was thinking this, but I wondered what it would feel like to be taken by two men at one time. I knew that it was something I would never do in real life, but still, it had been something that I had fantasized about.

As I laid on the bed, I began to think about Hawk and how much I missed him. Then I began to think about Victor and how attracted I was to him even though I shouldn't be. Rolling over on my side, I closed my eyes. The only thing I saw was Hawk and then Victor. *"How could I possibly be attracted to two men who were completely different from each other?"* I thought to myself. Reaching under the covers, I could feel the wetness of my panties as I slipped my hand underneath the silky fabric. I couldn't believe how aroused I was thinking about these two men. Spreading my slick folds with my index finger, I began gently rubbing my finger between them, feeling the pleasure that it made. With my thumb, I found my clit and began applying circular movements on the hard nub. My body began moving, grinding against the feel of my finger. Needing more, I dipped my finger inside my vagina.

There was only one thought in my mind: the fantasy I knew I would never experience in reality. Just the thought of being taken by two men at one time had my mind spinning and my body on fire. Continuing in my fantasy world, I placed the index finger of my other hand in my mouth, covering it with saliva, and lowered it to my nipple as I began swirling it around the taut peak. All I could see was Victor's mouth, sucking and licking my breast, while Hawk's mouth was on my pussy working wonders on my clit. Imagining being pleasured in this unheard of way had my body expelling the most intense release that it had ever felt. Feeling guilty for feeling such pleasure from a desire I knew I could never have, I rose from the bed and went to the shower to remove the remnants of my naughty thoughts. This experience, I knew, I would never be able to share with anyone.

CHAPTER TWELVE

Hawk

Tossing and turning, all I could think about was the way Paige looked when she and Nikki went through the back entrance of the bar. I wanted to take her right then. She was the most gorgeous woman I had ever seen. When I saw that guy walk over to her table while Nikki was playing pool, I just about lost it. I knew I needed to keep my cool, especially considering the last time a guy laid his hands on her. So just like a fly in a corner, I just sat back and watched. Whatever he was saying to her was making her face light up with delight. I wished that I could have gotten close enough to hear what was going on.

Unable to stand it anymore, I got up to get something to drink. It was killing me knowing that there might be another man that could give her more than I could. One thing I did know was that I needed to find out who this guy was. I was glad that I was smart enough to pull my phone out and get a quick picture of him. One way or another, I was going to find out who this guy was.

Knowing that sleeping would be a lost cause, I decided to get up and go for a drive. Maybe some fresh air would clear my head. Grabbing my keys, I headed out the door. Putting the Mustang in reverse, I backed out of the parking space and headed south to Boomer Lake. It was early in the morning and the sun still hadn't made its appearance. I knew that it was late enough that the lake should be fairly deserted. Most of the high school lovebirds should be long gone.

When I reached my favorite spot, I looked out the windshield and admired the moon shining on the glassy water. Everything was so different here. It was like being in a whole different world. No stress, no pressure, just me and the quietness. As I sat on the rock, everything began playing in my mind. From the time I was a teenager dealing with all the shit that happened, to when I was in Iraq, living yet another kind of hell. If it hadn't been for my brothers who served with me, I might have been a statistic just like all the other vets who either committed suicide or were committed to a nuthouse.

Then there was Paige, the one thing that I felt was good in my life. The only thing was, it felt like even that was slipping away. If she knew what I really desired, she would be gone forever. I needed to make sure that if I was going to take things to the next level with her, I didn't reveal what I truly wanted. What I truly craved.

Watching the sun come up in the distance, I decided I needed to get back to town. I was totally exhausted even though I was unable to sleep. That didn't change when I got back to the motel. My only other option was to take the one thing that I tried to avoid taking. Drugs weren't my thing, but when my body was beyond exhausted and I needed to have some rest, it was the only thing that would help. After popping two pills in my mouth, I stretched my body on the lumpy mattress and closed my eyes.

~****~

When I woke up the next morning, or rather afternoon, my head ached like I drank a full bottle of Jack. Even though the narcotic drug I took helped me sleep, I didn't like the way it made me feel when I woke. I didn't like not having a clear head. I wasn't sure what was the worst of the two evils, being totally exhausted or having a headache the size of the Grand Canyon.

Pushing from the bed, I headed to the bathroom for a cold shower. Maybe that would alleviate some of the pressure in my head. Stripping off my jeans and t-shirt, I turned on the water to the shower. As the cool water hit my body, I could already feel the pressure lessen. Now the only thing to worry about was the erection I was sporting. Thoughts of Paige had been the only thing on my mind from the minute I took the diazepam to when I woke up. Everything in between was a complete blank. All I knew was that she was the cause of the hardness of my cock. Lowering my hand, I wrapped it around the shaft and began stroking it up and down, trying to relieve the pressure that had been building. I wish that it had been Paige satisfying my urge to spill. Closing my eyes, I did the only thing I could do, relieve myself.

Once I finished with my task. I got dressed and headed out the door to Paige's place. It was a short drive from where I was staying. Pulling around Hell's Gate into the alley, I parked the Mustang at the foot of the steps leading to her apartment. Taking the steps two at a time, I knocked on her door and waited for her to answer. The only thing I could see was Nikki's face as she pulled back the curtain. Opening the door and stepping to the side, I tipped my head to her and asked, "Is Paige here?"

"Yeah, she's in her room. I'll go get her," Nikki replied.

"No problem, I know where it is at," I said.

Walking toward Paige's bedroom, I noticed the empty bottles of wine sitting on the small table in front of the couch. The girls must have had a fun time last night after they left the bar. Turning my head back to the short hall, I headed to her room. Knocking lightly on the door, I heard a faint, "Come in," from the other side. The minute I opened the door, I could smell the hint of jasmine and vanilla in the air. Paige wasn't in her room, which only meant she had to be in the bathroom. Trying not to step on the mounds of clothing that were spread across the floor, I made my way to the slightly opened door to the bathroom. Pushing the door open, my heart began to race as I took in the perfect scenery of Paige laying in a bath full of bubbles with some sort of gel mask across her eyes.

Hearing the creak of the door, she lifted the mask from her eyes and looked over at me. The expression on her face told me that she wasn't expecting to see me standing at the door. "What are you doing here, Hawk? Don't you know how to knock?" she said, surprised.

"I did knock, you told me to come in," I reminded her.

"Yeah, well, that was only because I thought you were Nikki. Can you please turn around while I finish?" she demanded, raising her hand and making a circle with her index finger.

As I began turning so my back was to her, a small smile framed my face as I thought how nice it would have felt to climb in that tub with her and give her what she wanted. There was a small chair in the corner of the room, which I turned and sat on with the back facing the door and my arms resting on it while I straddled the seat. Taking a deep breathe, I began my interrogation. "So, tell me how much you know about Nikki?"

"Why would you want to know about Nikki?" she asked, as the water began sloshing around her.

"Everything that has happened over the past couple of days began the minute she got to town. Seems kinda odd, don't you think?"

"If you are talking about that SUV that showed up at the lake, yeah, it seems kind of strange," she replied.

"It's not only that, Paige, It's the scene she caused with her shoulder. Did you know she is some sort of contortionist and that she wasn't hurt at all?" I argued.

"What are you talking about, Hawk? She was really hurt."

"No, not really. Spoke with the doc. Nikki is double jointed in her shoulder and was able to pop it out of place just long enough for us to think she was hurt," I admitted.

"I can't believe that," Paige countered.

"There is something you should know. The SUV that showed up at the lake belongs to some international diplomat. I had one of the guys check the plate number for me. Do you know if Nikki has any ties or family overseas?" I questioned.

I wasn't sure if Paige was surprised to hear what I just shared with her, or if she was thinking about her friend. "Paige, did you hear what I just said?"

"What? Yeah, I heard. There is no way she would or could be involved with anything like that. I personally think it was a coincidence. Maybe whoever was in the SUV was sightseeing or something," she replied.

I tried to keep my eyes peeled on the bathroom door as I heard Paige release the plug in the tub. I knew that soon she would be standing and her beautiful body would be on display. Taking a chance. I turned my head slightly, watching her climb out of the tub and hunt for a towel. Little did she know that it was currently under my ass. I knew I should have laid it on the counter so she could grab it and cover herself once she finished her bath, but I wanted to see that gorgeous body of hers. Lifting my ass from the chair. I picked up the towel and walked over to where she was still looking for it. With her back to me, I wrapped the towel around her small frame and spun her around. As we looked at each other, I could see the desire she had in her eyes. Moving a stray hair that had fallen over her eye, I lowered my head and gently kissed her on her soft lips. When her mouth opened, letting me in, I knew that she did indeed desire me and what I was offering. Swirling our tongues together in perfect unison, I deepened the kiss and clutched her tight ass in my hands, squeezing the creamy flesh.

There wasn't enough room in the bathroom to do

what I needed to do to her, so I lifted her body from the floor with my lips on hers and my hands clenched tight on her ass. I walked out of the bathroom to her bed, which was also covered in clothes. Releasing one hand from her body, I swung it across the bed, sending her clothes flying across the room. Placing her gently on the mattress, her eyes fell closed and I began unbuttoning my 501's. Paige's arms stretched above her head. God, how I wanted to tie them to the headboard at that moment. As I pulled down my jeans, I noticed a blue scarf on the floor just calling my name. Grabbing it, I went to the head of the bed, took hold of her wrists and wrapped the silky material around each wrist. Securing her to the spindles on the headboard, I took in the sight of her gorgeous body. Her breasts were pulled tight with her nipples at full attention, just waiting to be caressed.

Kneeling beside her, I lowered my head to her taut nipple and began kissing and sucking, making circular movements with the tip of my tongue. God, how I loved the sight of her breasts. So perfect in every aspect of the word. Feeling the arch of her back, I grabbed the condom that I laid on the nightstand before I grabbed the scarf. I wanted to worship her until every inch of her body was completely sensitized with my touch. Taking her by the ankles, I quickly flipped her body over, exposing her luscious ass. My hands slowly moved down her soft body until they reached the apex of her ass. Taking my index finger, I parted her cheeks and glided it down to the entrance of her vagina, where I found her hot and wet, ready to be taken. Not just yet though, I wanted to play with this tantalizing body just a little longer. Bringing my finger to my lips I stuck it in my mouth, tasting her, enjoying every drop of her sweet nectar. "God, you have the sweetest pussy I have ever tasted," I breathed as I finished cleaning my finger.

I could hear her moan into the pillow as her hips began rising off of the bed, sending her perfect ass my way. It took everything I had to hold back what I wanted to do to her body. Placing my finger between her folds, I once again lapped up her juices, spreading her sweet honey along her backside until I felt her tiny pucker. I wanted so badly to take her there, but I knew she wasn't ready. I was well blessed and I didn't want to hurt her. She needed to be prepared before I entered her tight ass. Leaning over her arched body, I whispered softly in her ear, "One day your tight little ass will be mine." With my finger still moving up and down her slick folds, I felt the onset of her release coating my already soaked finger. Finding her sweet entrance, I slipped my finger inside her, reveling in the tightness of her pussy as it gripped my finger.

I couldn't wait any longer. My cock was throbbing and needed attention before I exploded before I even had a chance to get me some of that hot pussy. Ripping the wrapper off the condom, I placed the lubricated latex over my cock and expertly rolled it on with one hand. This was something I perfected over the years. Being able to fuck a chick fast and hard gave me the inspiration to perfect that technique. Within seconds my cock was sheathed and pushing its way inside her. Making slow movements, I began working my dick inside her while my finger made circular movements around her anus. All I could think about was how nice it would be to have a butt plug in that tight ass of hers while fucking her tight pussy.

Pushing deeper inside her, her hips lifted higher. I needed to go deeper. Being in the perfect position, I reached around her body with my free hand and lifted her from the bed while commanding her, "Wrap your sexy legs around my waist, baby."

She did as she was told, giving me the deepest penetration possible. With each thrust of my cock inside her, I could feel the walls of her pussy tighten around me like a vice-grip. Every pull of my cock sent me to a whole new world as she held on to me, squeezing and pushing against me. "Oh God, baby, your pussy is driving me crazy," I yelled, feeling the juices of her vagina coat my hard cock. With her moans of release, I lost all control and spilled my own juices inside the confines of the latex rubber. Falling over her, I rested my head against her shoulder and listen as her breathing began to even out. I have fucked so many women in my lifetime, but none would ever compare to what she just gave me. Pure Heaven.

CHAPTER THIRTEEN

Paige

Looking around the room, I wasn't sure what got into me. My room looked like a tornado hit it. I must have pulled every article of clothing that I owned from my closet and my drawers. I still didn't find what I was looking for. Now more than ever, I needed to find it. After what Hawk said about the SUV, I knew it was only a matter of time before he would find out the real truth. Nikki had no ties to that SUV. It was just a coincidence that she showed up in Stillwater just about the time things started getting weird. I needed to let her know what was going on.

Pushing to my feet, I looked back over to Hawk, who was still sleeping like a baby. *"God, he's gorgeous,"* I thought to myself as I headed to the bathroom to relieve myself. When I finished, I went to the kitchen to begin brewing my fix of caffeine. Nikki was snoring away on the couch like an old man. I had never in my life heard such an awful sound come out of such a pretty face. With everything ready, I turned on the coffee maker and walked over to Nikki. Leaning over her. I pinched her nose with my thumb and index finger. I almost peed my pants when she started to slap air. I had never seen anything like in in my life.

Removing my fingers, I heard her gasp for air. I felt really bad the minute she sat up and a look of terror spread across her face. "Don't you ever, I mean ever, do that again, Paige," she yelled, spilling tears from her eyes.

"I'm so sorry, Nikki. I didn't think it was going to cause such a reaction in you. What is going on with you? I've never seen anyone react like that." I asked.

"Well, you would react like that too if someone cut off your air," she stated matter-of-factly.

Sitting next to her, I held out my hand and said,

"Truce."

I knew she forgave me as she reached out and shook my hand. Patting her on the knee, I advised, "Coffee's done. Do you want a cup?"

"Hell yeah, I want cup," she said.

Pushing up from the couch, I walked back to the kitchen and poured each of us a cup of Java. Walking back to her with two cups of coffee in hand, I handed her one and took a seat beside her. As she sipped her coffee, I knew this was as good a time as ever. "Hawk thinks that the SUV at the lake had something to do with you. He got information that it belonged to an international diplomat, which could only mean one thing. They found me." I started, taking a sip of coffee. "I need you to do me a favor, Nikki."

"What's that?" she asked.

"I need you to play along with what he believes. It's the only way he will stop digging into me. If he thinks it is you that is in trouble, maybe he will leave me alone."

"So you want me to pretend that I am the princess of Kierabali? I don't know one thing about being a princess, Paige. He is going to know right away that something isn't right. He is no dummy," she confessed.

"You let me worry about that. I will teach you everything you need to know about my life. You will know everything. There is no way he will figure this out."

"Okay, if you say so," Nikki began. "So, since I am going to be playing the part of your royal highness, don't you think I should be treated as such? Fill her up, slave," Nikki ordered while handing me her empty coffee mug.

Rolling my eyes at her, I stood and took her cup, Just as I turned away from the counter with her full cup of coffee, Hawk entered the small living area with his jeans only half zipped, revealing the '*V*' of his defined waist. I knew that my mouth dropped open, allowing anything to fly inside. Before I could compose myself, I head Hawk say, "Whose slave?"

Turning back toward the counter I replied, “How about a cup of coffee?”

As I pulled a cup down from the high cupboard, Hawk began walking closer to where I was. I felt like he was about ready to pounce on me like I was his prey the way he was coming at me with slow, calculated steps. Handing him his coffee, I asked in a soft tone, “Why are you coming at me that way?”

“Because you looked like you were about to bite my head off,” he said.

“Why would I do that?” I replied, still using the soft tone.

“You tell me?”

“Can we talk about this later when there aren’t so many ears in the corn field?” I said.

Taking his cup of coffee from me, Hawk headed

back in the direction of my bedroom. When I knew he was out of earshot, I looked over to Nikki and said, “Remember what I said.”

“Yeah, yeah, I know.”

~****~

I was thankful that the rest of the day wasn’t as eventful as the morning. I was also thankful that after Hawk took a shower he left, needing to take care of some stuff. I wasn’t even sure what he did at Jagged Edge Security. I guess it would have been a good idea to find out. The next time I saw him, I was going to make it a priority to ask exactly what he did for them. It was getting close to my shift at the bar and Nikki decided my small apartment needed some TLC. Cleaning wasn’t something that I got used to doing. Living in a palace with your own servant pretty much took away any need to pick up after yourself.

Entering the bar, Merrill was already at his usual spot behind the bar. Bucky was in the back loading a dolly with cases of beer. Heading to the bar, I saw a familiar face sitting at the far end. It was Victor. Tucking my belongings on a shelf under the register, I walked over to him to say "hello." Grabbing another beer, I headed his way. Placing the beer on the bar, I removed his empty bottle and said, "This one is on the house."

There was that amazing smile again. Leaning up against the bar, I watched as he took a swig of his beer. Without even thinking, I asked. "So what brings you here so early in the evening?"

"I knocked off early," he confessed.

Pretending to look busy, I began wiping down the bar surface. "So what is it you do exactly?"

"A little bit of this and a little bit of that," he replied.

I wasn't sure what a little bit of this or a little bit of that meant exactly, but by the way he was dressed, I would have to guess that he was a businessman of some sort. I began guessing in my head what he did for a living. "*Investment banker, nah. CEO of his own business, nah.*

Lawyer, nah." There were too many occupations that would require him to be dressed in a suit. My only option was to ask. "So where do you do a little bit of this and a little bit of that?"

"Everywhere, actually. I buy and sell property. If it's scllablc, I'm there," he confessed.

"Sounds like a very demanding job," I said.

"Nah, not really. I get to choose my own hours," he stated.

"Nice."

The bar was filling up pretty quickly and I needed to get back to work before I got slammed. Moving away from Victor with a smile, I began taking drink orders on the other end of the bar. There was something about Victor that seemed to be familiar. After seeing him again, I still couldn't pinpoint what it was. Although I did find him very attractive, there was still something that told me to beware of him.

As the evening wore on, more and more people came into the bar. By the time ten o'clock hit, the bar was pretty much standing room only. This was the first time I had seen it so packed since I began working here over a week ago. I knew that with this many people I would be making excellent tips, which also meant that the possibility of there being a fight increased. Bucky was a pretty big guy, but if a fight did break out, I doubted that he would be able to break it up. Keeping track of the amount of liquor I was selling, I noticed that we were getting low on vodka and JD. Letting Merrill know of our liquor situation, I headed to the back stock room to grab a couple of more bottles. When I can back to resume my position, Hawk was sitting at the end of the bar where Victor was sitting previously. It made me wonder what happened to him. He was there before I went to the back room. The only conclusion I had was that Hawk must have said something to him.

Walking to the end of the bar, I stared Hawk in the eyes and asked. "Okay, where did he go?"

Hawk looked at me like I was half nuts. "Where did

who go?" he asked.

"Don't act dumb, Hawk. You know exactly who I am talking about."

"Oh, you mean the loser that was just sitting here," he said. "He must have had a family emergency or something."

"Very funny, Hawk. It wouldn't have been you that convinced him to leave?" I asked, placing my hands on my hips.

"Me? No. Guy just took off."

For some reason, I didn't believe a word Hawk said. Knowing his drink of choice, I picked up the bottle of JD and poured him a double with a draft beer on the side. Placing it in front of him, I waited for him to pull out the twelve bucks needed to pay for the drinks. When he didn't move, I asked him straight out, "Tab?"

With a nod of his head, I went to the register and

entered his name. Having a tab was the preferred way of most of the patrons. The only problem was most of them skipped out before paying their bill. I kept telling Merrill that we should at least keep their credit card so that it could be run at the end of the night. He didn't want to hear about my suggestion. He was old school and trusted everyone to settle up their bill when the night was over. Anyone who didn't, Bucky always managed to get to them before they got too far out the door.

When two o'clock rolled around, I was more than ready to hit the sack. For it being a busy night, there wasn't much to clean up. I was glad when Merrill told me to take off and that he would handle the cleanup. I could have kissed the man. It wasn't like I wouldn't have stayed to help, but when someone offers to let you off early, you would have to be stupid not to accept.

CHAPTER FOURTEEN

Hawk

I may have been a little hard on the loser sitting at the end of the bar gawking at Paige like he was about to take what little clothing she had on off of her. As far as I was concerned, she was *my* girl and no one was going to have her. So when I told Victor or whatever his name was that someone ran into his Benz, he all but jumped out of his chair and rushed to the door. He was going to have a little surprise waiting for him when he got outside, especially seeing that his car was no longer parked across the street. I almost gave up hot-wiring the damn thing, but when I finally got it to start, there was no problem driving it four blocks over and parking it near a fire hydrant. With my luck, it would be ticketed and towed before he finally found it. So yeah, I guess you could say that he had an emergency to tend to.

Merrill was a hell of a guy to let Paige knock off early. Downing the rest of my drink, I walked behind the bar, where she was struggling to get the trash full of empty beer bottles out from under the counter. Placing my hand on her wrist, I took hold of the large metal can and picked it up and walked towards the back door of the bar. There was a large dumpster pushed against the brick wall. Swinging the can up, I easily dumped the contents inside. By the time I got inside, Mr. Loser was leaning against the end of the bar talking to Paige. So much for my little stunt I pulled. The way he looked, it didn't bother him at all. Walking behind the bar, I put the metal can back in its place and walked up behind Paige and placed my arms around her small waist. Kissing her cheek, I said loud enough for Mr. Loser to hear, "Are you ready to go, baby?"

Paige didn't stop me from kissing her or holding her close to me, at least not right away. Somehow she managed to get a good grip on my little finger and began to push it back, Damn, that girl was strong. Turning my way, she said very softly, "I know what you did, and no, I am not ready to leave yet, at least not with you."

I guess this was my cue to let her go. Lowering my head to her ear, I whispered softly, "I'll wait, then."

Paige released my finger and I moseyed to the other side of the bar where Merrill was already standing there with a beer and a shot of JD in his hand. He must have known that I would be waiting for Paige for a long time based on thc largc grin he had on his face. Taking the shot glass and draft from his hand, I moved to the other side of the bar and took a seat. Before I sat my ass down, I could feel the vibration of my phone in the back pocket of my jeans. As I swiped the screen, I could see that it was Peter calling me. I could also see that it was close to midnight.

"Hey, bro, what's up?" I asked.

"Got some more information on your situation down there. I think we may have been off base with thinking that Nikki may be in trouble. She has nothing to do with that SUV. The plate number you gave us from the Benz belongs to one Victor Walsh. He's been living in New York for the past six months. He's some sort of real estate man. He buys rundown properties and turns them into profit."

"Where was he before he lived in New York?" I asked.

"Nowhere in the States. I'm having Sly run an international check on him. Hopefully something will kick out on this guy," Peter advised.

"Wow, this shit just keeps getting thicker and thicker," I replied.

After I hung up with Peter, I looked over to the other end of the bar and stared at Paige and this other guy having a good old time. I could feel the tightness in my chest increase and the fingers on my hands clench into a fist. I wanted to beat this guy so bad, but knew it would be a mistake. So instead of going after him, I just stood there, fire rising in my blood, while Paige and he continued their little conversation. Just about ready to explode, I walked over to them and took Paige by the arm and walked her away from this loser. Facing her body towards mine, I said, "I think it's time to go, Paige."

As she pulled against my tight grip, I knew that she

was going to have marks on her arms. “Let me go, Hawk.”

There was no way I was ever going to be able to let her go. Lowering my shoulder, I slung her body over my shoulder and proceeded to the back exit. I could hear the sound of his footsteps behind me. Turning my body, I gave him onc look, making him hold up his hands in surrender and walk backwards a few steps before he turned around and went out the front door. I was so glad that he didn’t make a scene. The last thing I wanted was to lay this guy down and spend a night or two in jail. Right now my focus was on Paige and getting her to my place, where we would be alone with no interruptions.

The closer I got tot the back door the harder Paige began hitting my back with her closed fists. I knew that if she continued, she would be left with bruises on her knuckles. When I opened the door, I place her on the ground and held her by the wrist as she continued her assault on my body. “Paige, you need to stop. You’re going to end up hurting yourself,” I said.

“I don’t give a shit. You can’t just take me like that,

like I'm some sort of cave woman," she cursed.

Just when I thought she was done fighting with me, I let my guard down, only to feel the impact of her tiny fist come in direct contact with my jaw. I didn't realize that she could carry such a hard punch. Looking down on her, I could see her holding her hand and walking around in circles. I knew she really did it. She hurt herself. The one thing I didn't want to happen, happened. Trying to comfort her, I stopped her movements by wrapping my arms around her, only she was once again fighting me by swinging her arms like a madwoman.

When I finally had her where I wanted her, I placed her hands behind her back, holding them with one hand while I held her face with the other, Lowering my mouth, I kissed her with fire in my touch. There was no way I was going to be able to control the desire I had for her. Something in me snapped and my will to control her took over. She must have lost her own control, because no sooner than my lips were on hers, her mouth parted, allowing me to enter. Our tongues mingled with force like there was a shortage of want and we wanted it all. Lifting her from the ground, she wrapped her legs around my center as I walked us up the twelve steps to her apartment. My desire for her couldn't wait and her apartment was much closer.

As I held on tightly to her, she reached inside her small front pocket and pulled out her key. Seeing the trouble she was having with the lock. I took the key from her and slid it inside the keyhole, turned the knob, and pushed the door open. Our lips were still clenched together as I headed to her room. This time, I wasn't prepared to go slow with her. I wanted to take her my way. Taking the open sides of her button-up shirt in each hand, I pulled them apart, sending the buttons flying. Her chest was heaving with desire as I placed a kiss at the base of her cleavage, before lowering the cup of her bra and wrapping my mouth around her pert nipple. Her head fell back as I lowered the other cup and began kneading her soft mound in my hand.

When I looked up to her, I could see the desire for me she had in her eyes. I didn't even unhook the clasp in the front of her bra. I needed her bra off now, and with a quick, hard pull the bra came undone and was off of her in seconds, exposing her beautiful breasts. Pushing her shoulders slightly, her body fell to the bed, allowing me to remove the rest of her clothes. Unbuttoning her jean shorts, I pulled them down her legs along with her lacy white panties until they fell to the floor. God, she looked so beautiful lying there waiting for me to feast on her.

Pulling my belt off, I held it out and commanded, "Put your hands out, Paige."

Without so much as a word, she held out her hands like the little submissive she was born to be. Wrapping the leather around her wrist, I left enough on the end so I could secure it to the bed. With her hands high above her head, my cock was well on its way to exploding. Taking her by the ankles, I flipped her body over and lifted her tight ass in the air. With the palm of my hand, I planted a slap on her ass. The curve of her spine arched as I planted another slap, only this time a little harder. "One day this ass is going to be mine," I said between gritted teeth.

When I was satisfied that her ass was just the right

shade of pink, I rolled Paige over once again. Slipping my fingers between her folds, I lapped up her juices and held them to her mouth. “I want you to taste how much you loved being spanked.”

When her lips parted with no hesitation to my demand, I knew then that she was a true submissive and soon she would be under my control. No one would ever have her sweet pussy but me. Watching her lick and suck her juices from my finger was the most sensual thing I had ever seen. The way her lips wrapped around me, I couldn’t wait to feel them on my cock. Her mouth was perfect. Pulling my finger from her mouth, I leaned over her and whispered, “I’m so fucking hard for you, baby. I’m going to slip my dick inside that sweet little cunt of yours and fuck you until you scream my name.”

I positioned my throbbing shaft between her slick folds and began circling the outer edge of her entrance. Hearing her moans of pleasure I thrust my hips a little harder, sending her body reeling with desire. “I’m clean, baby. I need to feel all of you. Are you on the pill?” I asked in a breathy tone.

Her head nodded up and down, assuring me that she was on the pill. Rotating my hips, I placed my hands on her knees and spread her legs further apart. With her pussy fully exposed, I pushed inside, inching my way deeper and deeper inside her. When her back arched off the mattress, I felt every inch of her beautiful cunt as it tightened around my hard shaft. God, how I loved the feel of her as she tightened her muscles every time I pulled out of her. Lowering my head, I placed my mouth on her taut nipple and took the hard bud between my teeth and gently but firmly began applying a little pressure to the tip. Her back lifted even higher off the bed as I moved my cock harder and faster in and out of her. When my name fell from her lips, I knew then that she was mine.

CHAPTER FIFTEEN

Paige

Feeling the heat of his body next to mine, I slowly opened my eyes, feeling something that I have never felt before. The way Hawk took me last night, I wanted more. I wasn't the kind of person to submit to any man, but with him and the power he had in his voice, I wanted to give him everything that I had. Rolling over to my side, I threw the covers off my body and looked down at the new me. Everything was the same except for the tiny bruising around my upper arms and the slight redness of my nipples that were still hard. With my body exposed to the cool air, I decided to get up and shower. Careful not to wake Hawk, I swung my legs over the edge and slowly pushed off from the bed. Looking back over to Hawk, he was still out. I could have stared at him forever.

As I stood in front of the mirror, there was a slight tingle between my legs. I kept wondering if my relationship with Hawk would remain the way that it was, uncomplicated, or would things change? He still didn't know my secret and I didn't want what I was hiding to ruin what we had. As I began brushing my teeth, I heard a light knock on the door, before it slowly opened. Standing in all his glory was the man who showed me so much. Watching him walk up behind me, the wetness began to pool between my legs. Hawk's arms wrapped around me as he lowered his mouth to my shoulder and began placing soft kisses on my sensitized skin. When he hit just below my earlobe, he softly whispered, "Good morning, babe, how about a shower?"

I couldn't say 'no' to something so sexy. Turning my body so that I was facing him, I pushed to my tiptoes and gave him a light kiss on the lips, which ultimately ended up being a kiss of all kisses as he placed his hand on the back of my neck and held me close. The way he controlled me was something I thought I would never let a man do, but with Hawk it was different. It felt right.

Wrapping my arms around his shoulders, his grip on my neck lessened and his hands found the globes of my ass where he lifted me from the floor. Just like primal instinct, my legs found their place around his waist and my ankles locked.

Holding me close to him with one arm, Hawk reached inside the shower and turned on the water. With our lips still clinched to one another's, I stepped inside only to be blasted with cold water. “Jesus, holy mother of God, that’s cold,” I said with a shriek.

“Sorry, baby. I thought it was hot enough,” Hawk said with a laugh.

Turning my body away from the cold water, he took the brunt of the it until he was sure it was hot enough. Such a gentleman. Setting me on the tile floor, Hawk reached for the soap and began lathering it on the sponge. When it was fully lathered he began gently rubbing it down my body, first starting at my shoulders and then down toward my breasts. It didn’t surprise me that he stopped and gave this part of my body extra care. Rinsing the soap from my body, he lowered his head and began sucking and licking the hard peaks of my nipple. Even in the shower, he made my body wet with desire. Forking my hands through his hair, I held him close, not wanting him to stop. Moving from one side and then the other, both breasts had just received the tender loving care they needed.

Once again my feet were off the floor as Hawk pressed my body against the cold tile wall. In an instant his mouth was on mine, lacing his tongue with mine. It didn't take long until my body gave in to his touch and all my pleasure was released. Even Hawk knew what he had done to me. With a slight nudge, he was inside me, slowing inching his way deep inside. It was only after the third thrust that my body surrendered and the gates opened once more. With a heated breathe, he said, "We're going to need to work on your control, baby."

I wasn't sure what he meant by that. All I knew was that I wanted more of whatever he was giving. As my eyes closed, taking him in, his hand came to my cheek. I opened my eyes to see his beautiful hazel eyes staring back at me. "What is it, Hawk?" I asked with concern.

"I need to ask you something, baby," he began. With a nod of agreement, he resumed. "I need to know how you felt last night. I need to know if you were okay with what I did to you."

"I loved everything you did to me," I confessed. "It was like nothing I have ever experienced before."

I didn't know how he could do this now. Right in the middle of having sex. Whatever he was doing, though, I didn't want him to stop. His thrusts began getting harder and faster. My body was on its way to another mind-blowing orgasm.

"There are so many things that I want to show you, Paige. Things that you never knew your body could feel," he said, thrusting deeper and harder inside me. "I am going to fuck you in every way possible, even your body won't know what hit it."

The minute those declarations spilled from his lips, my body once again exploded beyond belief. Never have I had multiple orgasms. Then again, never had I been with a man like Hawk.

"You are going to come for me one last time, baby, only this time if you do it before I command you too, your tight little ass will be glowing with the sexiest shade of red."

Clinching my inner walls as tight as I could to stop the imminent release that was ready to erupt, I looked into Hawk's eyes and concentrated on the magnificent color and waited for his command. Thrust after thrust, the control not to come was to the point of unbearable. I wasn't sure that I could hold on much longer. The urge was beginning to take over. With a soft mother-may-I, I pleaded, "Please, Hawk."

"My darling Paige, come," echoed off the shower walls as my need to release took over.

As Hawk continued pushing deeper inside me, my juices continued to release, coating his cock. It was when I heard his moan of pleasure that I knew he also came like thunder, spilling his seed inside me.

~****~

An hour later Hawk and I were out of the shower and headed to the diner to satisfy the appetite we worked up. As we walked to the entrance, a woman about my age, holding the hand of a young boy, camc up behind us calling the name "Jayce." I wasn't sure who she was calling for until I looked around to notice the only male in the vicinity was Hawk. Stopping at the top of the steps, Hawk turned to face the woman. I knew that they knew each other just by the way she was looking at him. Turning his head towards me he said, "Go on in, I'll be right there."

"What is this about, Hawk?" I asked.

"Paige, please. Let me deal with this and I'll be in."

"Fine," I said, none to happy, and swung open the door to the diner.

I had no idea who this woman was, but Hawk definitely knew her and she knew him. Taking a seat at a booth right by the window I looked out to see if I could at least figure out what was going on. Even though I couldn't hear what they were talking about, I could at least see that whatever it was, it was pretty heated. I felt sorry for the little boy, who was now standing behind her. The more I watched the little boy the more it became evident. He could have been Hawk's little brother or… "Oh my God," I blurted out, forgetting where I was. Looking around the diner, everyone inside had their eyes peeled my way. Tipping my head, I said an embarrassed, "Sorry," and focused my eyes once again on what was happening outside.

The conversation between the woman and Hawk didn't last too much longer as she walked away from him. The last thing I saw was Hawk raking his hands through his hair before he climbed the steps of the diner. When he spotted me and saw the look on my face, his eyes immediately went to the ceiling. He knew that he had some explaining to do.

I was in no mood to wait. The minute he took a seat across from me, I crossed my arms at my chest and said,

"Spill."

"Nothing to say, Paige. Erica was a girl I used to know. It was a long time ago," he explained.

"Don't you see it?" I asked.

"See what?" he replied with a confused look on his face.

"That little boy, Hawk. He looks like a smaller version of you."

"You're crazy, Paige. He looks nothing like me," he said defensively.

"What are you not telling me, Hawk?"

"I'm not talking about this, Paige. Can we please just drop it and order breakfast?"

With a huff, I picked up the menu and looked at it, not seeing anything. After staring at it for what seemed like an eternity, I realized that the waitress was standing at the end of the table tapping her foot on the linoleum floor. With a boiling temperature, I said, “Two eggs over easy, wheat toast, and two slices of bacon, please.”

CHAPTER SIXTEEN

Hawk

I couldn't even believe this was happening to me. The last person I expected to see was Erica. And to top it all off, seeing her while I was with Paige. I had no idea the shit storm that was about to hit the fan. After all this time, now she wanted to talk about what we had. After I had just experienced the best fucking sex of my life. What a blow. Sure, what Erica and I had was out of this world, but that was a long time ago and I have moved on. The minute I told her no, I knew I was going to get my earful, but to threaten to tell Paige about us, that was the lowest of lows. The only thing I could do was agree to meet her later and pray I could convince her that she needed to move on.

Walking into the diner, Paige's face said it all. She

was pissed. I hated treating her the way I did, but I really needed her to leave it alone, at least until I could figure this out. By the time we left the diner. I could see the tension in Paige's body. I needed to do something to tame down the anger she had for me blowing her off. Grabbing her hand, I pulled her close to me, giving her a kiss she would never forget. She was mine and this was one way to let her know just that.

At first, I thought that she was going to give in and let me have my way with her, only that didn't happen. No sooner than my lips were on her, hers were off. The way she was looking at me, I knew I was in for something. Pointing her finger at me and stabbing it in my chest, she said in a raised voice, "If you think we are okay with what just happened, you are so wrong."

"Paige," I said sweetly. "Don't be like that, baby."

"Don't you dare 'baby' me, Hawk," she snapped with her finger still jabbing at my chest. "Matter of fact, you can just leave. I'll find my own way back to Hell's Gate.

When she started walking away, it was all I could do not to stare at that magnificent ass. I knew she was seriously pissed, but all I could do was smile at her. Damn, she was hot when she got mad. Walking to her in double time, I grabbed her by the arm and spun her body around. This was becoming a regular thing with us as I lifted her and slung her over my shoulder with very little effort. Once again the pounding of her fists on my back began, which brought another smile to my face, which I was glad she couldn't see. The last thing I wanted was to make her madder than she already was.

"Damn you, Hawk, put me down this minute. Do you hear me?" she spat.

"Not a chance, doll. Not until you cool your jets," I advised.

"Urrr… you are so alpha-male."

"You got that right, babe."

Once we reached my car, I hit the key bob and opened the passenger side door. Ducking my head, I lowered her body and carefully sat her on the leather seat. I was thankful that she didn't fight me by trying to get out. Latching her seat belt, I took the opportunity to kiss her on the cheek while I had the chance. *"So far so good,"* I thought to myself as I closed the door. Rounding the front of the car, I got in and started the car. From the corner of my eye, I could see Paige was still pissed. Her breathing was heavy as I watched her chest inflate and deflate with such force I thought she was going to pop the buttons of her shirt. Putting the car in reverse, I backed away from the diner and began heading towards town to Hell's Gate.

On the ride there, not one sound came from Paige. She was pissed even after I took the scenic route to the bar, hoping it would give her time to cool off. Turning into the alley, Paige had her seat belt unfastened before I could bring the car to a stop. Her door flew open the minute I stepped on the brake and put the car into neutral. For being such a little thing, she was awfully quick. Taking the steps leading to her apartment two at a time, she still wasn't quick enough for me. Just as she reached her door, my foot was there to stop it from being shut in my face.

"Go away, Hawk," she said.

"I'm not leaving you like this. We are going to talk this out," I said.

"Yeah, well, you made it perfectly clear you didn't want to talk about it at the diner."

"Paige, baby, Let me in," I pleaded.

It must have done the trick. The pressure of the door against my foot lessened and her angry, but beautiful face came into view. Before walking past her, I swept my hand along her cheek and lowered my mouth to hers. Her head turned before our lips met, letting me know she was still upset. Waiting until she shut the door, I leaned my body against the kitchen counter.

"Okay, so explain," she said, crossing her arms on her chest.

"The girl I was talking to was an old girlfriend from a long time ago," I began, hoping I could convince her there was nothing between Erica and I. "She is only a friend, Paige. Nothing more."

"What did she want?" Paige asked.

"She just wanted to catch up. Thought we could get together later," I said, telling only half of the reason.

"The little boy with her. Is he yours?"

"No, definitely not." I shot back. The little guy did look an awful lot like me, but there was no way he could have been mine. We were always careful during our sessions together.

"Did you sleep with her?" she asked with an unhappy look.

"She was my girlfriend, Paige. What do you think?"

"Then how can you be sure he isn't yours?"

"Because he's not," I started as I pushed from the counter. "Come here, beautiful."

With a little hesitation, Paige finally uncrossed her arms and walked towards me. When she was inches from me, I reached out and pulled her closer. As she gave me a little resistance, I lifted her head so that her eyes were in line with mine. "Paige, Erica is the past. You are with me now. I don't care about anyone else. Only you."

Her eyes were watery as I looked into them. There was something there. I wasn't sure what, but I could see that she was hurt. Lowering my lips to her, I took her with a kiss like no other. The last thing I wanted was for her to be sad, and think that I wanted any other woman but her. If someone would have asked me a week ago if I could ever be with one woman, I would have told them, "Fuck no."

When her lips parted to let me in, I knew I was forgiven. Picking her up, I set her on the counter. "Lift your arms, baby," I whispered as I took the bottom of her shirt and lifted it over her head. Her beautiful breasts heaved in front of me as I unfastened the front clasp of her bra. As she lowered her arms I moved her straps down her arms until she was free from the lace. With her breasts fully exposed, I took the taut peak of her nipple into my mouth and began sucking and kissing until her moans of pleasure filled the air.

I was so hard for this woman and needed to be deep inside her. Lifting her butt from the counter, I removed her shorts in one swoop, placing her just to the edge of the hard surface. As I held her with one arm, I worked on releasing my cock from the tight confines of my jeans. Once I was free, I began working my erection between her slick folds to the entrance of her tight channel. As I pushed inside her, I whispered with a heated breath, "I am going to show you so many things, baby, that your body won't know any other pleasure than what I am going to give you."

"Yes, please. Show me, Hawk. Show me everything," she breathed.

"I will, baby. Believe me, I will."

Paige had no idea what she was in for. I was going to show everything. Pulling her from the counter, I held her tight as I pushed my cock deeper and deeper inside her. Spinning her around, I held her body against the wall, thrusting harder while holding on to her. The only thing that I wished was that I had her strapped to a spanking bench so I could redden that beautiful ass of hers.

Gripping her hips, I pulled her tight little ass back as I pushed my hard cock inside her. Her hands were pressed against the wall, supporting her body as she pushed against me, giving more of herself to me. God, I loved the way her pussy felt wrapped around me. “That’s it, baby. Take me in,” I said, so close to my release.

“Hawk, I can’t hold on any longer. Please, I need to come,” she moaned.

“Not yet, baby. Remember control.”

I couldn’t expect her to reel in her control since I too was having a hard time holding back. Moving my hands from her hips, I placed them on her breasts and began tweaking her nipples to hard peaks. Her back began to arch and her release took over as I felt her juices coat my throbbing dick.

It wasn't long before my own self-control took off and I spilled inside her tight channel. Feeling the pressure finally subside, I pulled from her. I watched as the remnants of our juices began spilling from her pussy. It was the sexiest thing I had ever seen. Spinning her around so that she was facing me, I placed my hand on her cheek and kissed her softly. Breaking away, I said, "Shower."

"Yeah, you get it ready, I'll be right there," she said.

Kissing her again, I headed to the bathroom to get the shower water nice and hot. Waiting for a few minutes, I stuck my hand under the stream to make sure it was the right temperature. Satisfied, I yelled, "Baby, are you coming?" Waiting to hear her response, there was no reply. I didn't know what could be keeping her, so I headed out of the bathroom to check up on her. When I got to the living area, my confusion took over. The door was wide open and

Paige was nowhere to be found. Finding my jeans, which were lying on the kitchen floor, I pulled them on, thinking that she must have left. When I got to the open door, she wasn't there. "What the hell?" I said, scanning the alley for any sign of her.

Jogging down the steps, I ran around the corner of the building, hoping I would see her. Damn, the hard surface was killer on my feet. Looking up, I saw the back end of a black SUV turning right and heading down the street. Trying to gauge what was going on, I ran back to where my car was parked. Reaching inside my pocket, I didn't feel my keys. "Fucking hell," I cursed. Heading back up the steps back to her apartment, all I could think about was where the hell she would be going and what the hell was going on.

I had no idea where the black SUV was going. My only option was to take a right and hope that I hadn't wasted too much time and I would be able to see the SUV down the street. Stillwater wasn't very big, so I was pretty confident that I would find it.

Getting in my car, I started the engine and began backing up. Something was wrong. Putting the car in neutral and pulling up the hand break, I got out. “Fuck, fuck, fuck,” I cursed, seeing that both of my back tires had been slashed. With no other option, I pulled my cell from my pocket.

“Bro, I need your help.”

CHAPTER SEVENTEEN

Paige

After the explosive sex I just had with Hawk, I was ready for a hot shower to tame down the tingling he left my body in. Just as I finished getting a glass of water, there was a knock at the door. Putting on Hawk's t-shirt and my shorts, I quickly went over to answer it. I knew I should have looked to see to see who it was before opening the door. I didn't even have time to scream before one of the men had his hand over my mouth while the other one helped get me out of the apartment. I wasn't sure that Hawk would have been able to hear me anyway once he turned on the shower. I had a pretty good idea who these men were and what they wanted. What I didn't expect when they opened the door to the SUV was to see a man who wasn't who he said he was.

“Victor, what is going on?” I asked confused.

“Don’t you know, Isabelle? I’m here to claim what is rightfully mine,” he answered.

“I am not yours, Victor, nor will I ever be,” I advised.

“That, Isabelle, is where you are wrong.”

As one of the two men pushed me inside the SUV, I looked at Victor with disgust. I knew that arguing with him wasn’t going to earn me any brownie points. The only thing that I could hope for was that Hawk would realize I was gone before it was too late. Sitting back in the seat, I turned my body to look out the back window. There was no sign of Hawk, which basically told me that I was screwed.

“He isn’t coming for you. Clyde took care of that. Didn’t you, Clyde?” he asked.

“Yes, sir.” the man I assumed was Clyde answered.

"Yep, I'm definitely screwed," I thought to myself. Facing forward, I asked the one question I was afraid to know the answer to. "Where are we going, Victor?"

"Back to Kierabali, where you belong."

"You know this is kidnapping?" I cursed.

"Not in the eyes of the Kierabalian people. As far as they know, I am rescuing you from a dangerous man," he replied with a grin.

"What are you talking about, Victor?" I asked, afraid of what he was going to say.

"Oh, I'm sorry, Isabelle, didn't you know? Your little boyfriend is a wanted man in Kierabali. I am going to be a hero saving you, the Princess of Kierabali, from such a dangerous man," he bragged.

"You're crazy. They are never going to believe you. When I tell them the truth, it will be you that they will find is dangerous," I vowed.

"That is where you are wrong, Isabelle. You will be too distraught. The people will understand your confusion."

There was no way that Victor was going to get away with this. I just needed to figure how I was going to be able to get away from him. The last thing I wanted was to go back to Kierabali and be under the control of him, or any other man, for that matter. I was pretty sure that my uncle also had something to do with bringing me back. He, of all people, had the most to gain.

As we continued driving, I kept thinking about what was going on in Stillwater. I knew that by now Hawk would have noticed that I was gone. With all the resources he had, certainly he would be able to find me. It was then that I remembered that he really had nothing. All of his information pointed to Nikki. The way she played him at the lake, why wouldn't he believe she was in trouble? If I knew Nikki, she would never tell Hawk the truth about me. She would rather be tortured than to say anything that was sworn in the holiest of holy ways according to her.

Heading out of the small town, I knew that we were heading in the wrong direction in order to go back to New York. Turning on a dirt road, a small airport came into view. On the side of the road was a small sign displaying the words "Stillwater Regional Airport." I had no idea that the small town even had an airport. Feeling my heart drop inside my stomach, I knew that my time in this little town was over. I would be going back to the life that I didn't want. Circling around the small building, the tarmac came into view. The SUV pulled to a stop in front of a private jet with the Kierabalian seal on the side of the plane. I recognized the seal right away. As I was assisted out of the SUV, I looked up the steps leading inside the plane to find my uncle standing at the doorway to the jet. He was dressed in a black suit and a crisp white shirt.

The closer I got to the small plane, the better I could see the smirk on his face exhibiting his arrogant demeanor that I hated so much. As I walked towards him with his security on each side of me, I began feeling nauseated at what was in store for me. Looking up to him, he said with a sarcastic tone, "So glad you could join us, Isabelle."

"Why are you doing this, Maxwell?" I questioned.

"Because it is your birthright and you need to take responsibility for what was handed down to you," he answered.

"This isn't about my birthright, uncle. I'm pretty sure this is more about what you have to gain by bringing me back," I hissed, my hands fisted at my sides.

"Now, now, Isabelle, no need to be nasty. Whether you like it or not, you are going to be Princess of Kierabali and Victor will be standing at your side as Prince. It has been all arranged and not even your boyfriend can stop it," he remarked.

I knew he was right. As much as I hated having to go back, the odds of escaping were stacked against me. With his two guards, Victor, and himself, there was no way I would be able to get away from them. Just walking past him, I entered the plane and took a seat on the leather chair next to the window. At that moment, I could feel the tears beginning to form. I had to be strong. I couldn't let him know that he finally tore me down. I didn't care what it took, I was going to find a way out of this. When I did, he would never be able to find me again.

~****~

Four hours into our flight, we landed in a remote area to refuel. I had no idea where we were, only that I was even more angry than I was before. Even though the flight attendant tried to make me as comfortable as possible, it still didn't tame down the resentment I had for my Uncle Maxwell. As I looked over to him, I couldn't believe how very different he and my father actually were. Even though they shared pretty much the same features, which included the gentle blue eyes and the strong jaw line, my uncle was nothing like my father. If he was alive today, my father never would allow this to happen. He would want me to do what made me happy. He would never allow me to be transported back to a country that I didn't want to be in, no matter what my birthright was.

The plane took off again once it was fully fueled. I

heard chatter that the plane would need to refuel at least one more time before making a permanent landing in Kierabali. I knew that there was another four hours until the next stop. I thought this was as good time as any to get some sleep. Pulling the handle on the side of the leather chair, I put it in a reclining position. Adjusting my body, I closed my eyes and tried to get some rest. The noise around me faded and I was soon asleep.

"Princess Isabelle Moraco, do you accept this man, in the eyes of the Kierabalian people, to rule this land beside you as your Prince and husband?" the chancellor asked of me.

"Yes, with all my heart," I replied.

Was that me saying those words? I would never marry a man like Victor. He can't be trusted. As I looked over to the man I was to spend the rest of my life with, I realized that it wasn't Victor at all. Instead, it was a man that I wanted to share the rest of my life with. Hawk. It was Hawk standing before me. As I looked into his piercing eyes, I knew then that he was the man I wanted forever.

Wait, what was happening? Why were those men coming down the aisle? Why would they ruin this very special day for me? Taking Hawk by the arms, they began pulling him away from me.

"Wait! Stop!" I yelled, trying to pull him back to me.

It didn't matter how hard I tried, the harder I pulled on him the further from my grasp he got. "No, you can't take him away from me. Please don't take him from me."

There was a sudden drop in altitude, which instantly woke me from my nightmare. I knew that the way Victor and Maxwell were looking at me, they heard my plea. Even though it was only a dream, it was one that I didn't want to share with them. The plane dropped again, causing me to grip the armrest of the leather chair. Looking out the window, I could see that the clouds had turned from blue to gray. We were heading straight into a storm. I knew exactly what that meant. The smaller the plane, the less likely it would survive a storm of this magnitude. I was beginning to feel sick as the small jet began rocking back and forth. I usually wasn't the type of person that got motion sickness, but the way the plane was swaying, it was more than I could handle. Reaching over my lap, I caught the seat beat and fastened it over me. Just as the belt clicked. I heard the pilot's voice come over the speaker.

"The is some unsettling weather up ahead. I would ask that you remain in your seats and fasten your seat belts," he commanded.

He certainly didn't have to ask me twice. Looking over to my uncle and Victor, I could see that they were as concerned as I was, if not more. The weather must have gotten worse, because the swaying and bobbing of the little plane began to increase. There wasn't anything I could see out the window to let me know exactly how bad it actually was. Everything was either gray or white. Once in a while I could see a burst of light, which could only be lightning. I had never been so afraid in my life. The plane dipped again, only this time it continued downward. I could feel the pressure on my body as it was being pushed back into the seat. I did everything I could to adjust my position, but the force prevented me from doing so. I knew something was wrong. The pilot should have been able to even out by now. Just then I heard a snap and knew this was the end. “Oh God, please help me.”

CHAPTER EIGHTEEN
Hawk

I had never been so pissed in my life. Not only did they slash two of my tires, but I forgot to replace the spare tire I had in my trunk. The last thing I wanted was to call a tow truck to haul my Mustang to the shop to get not only two tires replaced, but the one in the trunk as well. I could feel the tension in my face, knowing how much this was going to cost me. As I waited for the shop mechanics to replace my tires, I needed to think about something else to occupy my mind. I knew it was going to take Peter and Sly some time to get here. Thinking about Paige, I pulled my phone from my pocket to call Nikki, but remembered that I didn't have her number. Walking back in the garage, I went to the office to see how long it would be until they had my car ready.

After talking with the mechanic, I was told forty-five minutes to an hour, tops. This was not what I wanted to hear. The more time that passed, the more my chances of finding Paige lessened. At least the garage was within walking distance to Paige's apartment. If I hurried I could be there in five minutes.

When I got to Paige's apartment, the door had been shut with the curtain pulled open, which let me know that Nikki was back and inside. Pounding on the door with my fist, I waited for her to answer. When she opened the door, I pushed past her. "I need some answers and I need them now, Nikki," I cursed, not giving her the chance to close the door on me.

"What the hell, Hawk? Paige isn't here," she said.

"I know that, I think she was taken. The same SUV that showed up at the lake showed up here less than an hour ago." I began swiping my hand through my already tousled hair. "If you know anything, you need to spill."

“Oh God,” she said with concern.

“Nikki, tell me what you know,” I demanded.

“I can’t, Paige made me promise not to say anything.”

“Nikki, so help me… I don’t have time for this shit. She could be in a lot of trouble,” I reminded her.

“Okay, okay, jeez. Paige thought those men at the lake were after her. She thinks her uncle may have sent them. God, she is going to kill me,” Nikki said, pacing the floor. “She’s some sort of princess from one of those little islands. She ran away because she was supposed to marry some diplomat's son whom she had never met. I guess it was prearranged when she was still in diapers or something like that.”

“You’ve got to be shitting me,” I said with disbelief.

“Nope. My guess is if she is gone, they are the ones

who took her."

"Do you have any idea where?" I asked, perturbed.

"Shit, Hawk, I can't remember. Some island."

"That doesn't help me, Nikki. Do you know how many islands there are?"

I knew I made Nikki feel bad about not knowing the name of the island that Paige was taken to. I still couldn't digest what she had told me. Who would have ever thought that Paige would be a princess? It made sense, though. It was like she hadn't existed before twelve months ago. At least now I had something to go on.

Heading back to the serviced station, I called Peter to let him know the information I had on Paige. Maybe he could work that magic of his and figure out who she really was. If I had to guess, I bet her real name wasn't even Paige Harper. As I entered the station, I could see that the mechanics were putting the last tire on my car. Settling back in the corner of the garage, I watched them finish up and then lower the car off the jack. One of the mechanics walked over to me, handing me my keys and a bill for the work they did. Looking at the bill, I just about lost it. I don't know what they were thinking, but those tires were not made out of gold like the bill reflected. Twelve hundred dollars later, I was out of the garage and out of cash.

Driving back to the motel, I knew that Peter and Sly would be showing up any minute. I needed some down time to get my head on straight and figure out what to do. Just as I pulled up to the motel, I saw that the door to my room was open. I only prayed that this wasn't a repeat from the other day. Walking back to my car. I went to the glove box and pulled out my handy friend from the compartment. Taking cautious steps to the open door, I drew my gun, prepared to shoot anything that moved. Squatting low, I peeked around the corner of the door, to see that Peter and Sly were inside. "Jesus fucking Christ, you guys couldn't have waited for me outside?" I cursed.

"Didn't want to draw any attention. When you called you sounded like a crazy man," Peter answered.

"Yeah, well, I was, still am. You guys aren't going to believe what I'm about to tell you," I said, taking a seat at the small table while Peter and Sly remained on the bed.

Going through every detail that Nikki told me and leaving nothing out, I could tell that Peter and Sly were just as shocked as I was when I first heard the news. Who would have thought that my little angel would be a princess? Of all things, a fucking princess. I wasn't sure where to begin to look for information on her. There wasn't really very much to go on other than she was the princess of some island in the South Pacific. I wasn't even sure how many islands there were out there. Looking over to Peter, I saw a serious look on his face, like his mind was working a mile a minute. Before I could ask him what was on his mind, he stood and went to a bag that was on the floor in front of the bed.

As he unzipped the bag, he said, "I've got an idea." Pulling his laptop from the bag, he sat back down on the bed. "If she was some sort of princess, there would have been something about her going missing twelve months ago."

I had to agree with Peter. There was no way a missing princess wouldn't have hit the news. Taking a seat beside him, I waited while his computer booted. With the mobile hot spot app on his phone, he connected the Wi-Fi and began his search. It was a matter of a couple of clicks before the news popped up *'Princess Isabelle Moraco of Kierabali goes missing'* in the search engine results. When Peter clicked on the link, a paged open reveling not only a picture of Paige, but also a picture exactly like the one I had found in her wallet. Scrolling further down the page, there was an article regarding the death of her parents and how some Maxwell Moraco was given guardianship over her and all her assets. It also stated that she was to marry a Victor Walsh, who was chosen at birth to be her husband and the new Prince of Kierabali. Everything I was reading was so messed up. Who in their right mind would want to marry someone they didn't know?

The good side of this messed up story was at least we knew who she really was and where she more than likely was taken. We just needed to figure out how we were going to get to her. At least that is what I was thinking.

Peter had a whole different look at the situation.

“Well, so much for that, bro,” Peter said, closing the lid on his laptop.

“What are you talking about, Peter?” I asked.

Looking at me with confusion, he replied, “You need to let this go, Hawk. There is no way the Kierabalian government is going to let us just waltz in and bring her back to the States. It isn’t even certain that she wants to come back here.”

“Are you serious, Peter? No one comes to the States, changes their name, and lays low for twelve months just for shits and giggles. There is a reason she left Kierabali and changed her name. It’s because she didn't want to be found,” I cursed.

“You’re nuts, Hawk. You need to let this go,” Peter commanded, rising to his feet and stuffing his laptop back in his duffel bag.

“You know what, Peter, I don’t need your fucking help. Matter of fact, why don’t you both just go back to New York?” I was so pissed. I couldn’t believe, of all the people in the world, that Peter would back away from helping me.

“Come on, Sly, let’s get out of here,” Peter zipped his bag and slung it over his shoulder. Just when I thought he was done, he turned his body toward mine. “Don’t do anything stupid, Hawk.”

As they both went out the door, Sly reached over and patted my shoulder. The look he gave me said it all. He knew how I felt, only his hands were tied. He would be stupid to go against Peter’s wishes. Giving him a slight nod, letting him know I knew how he felt, I watched as they walked away. Within minutes of letting them leave, a yellow cab pulled up and both of them got in. I still couldn’t believe that they left like that. Whatever happened to the ‘one for all and all for one’ pact?

I was alone in this, so I needed to get a plan in order. I just didn’t know what the hell that was going to be.

I just knew that I had never felt more for a woman than I did for Paige, or Isabelle, or whatever her name was. All I knew was, I was falling for her and I couldn't see being without her in my life. I was going to do whatever it took to get her back.

CHAPTER NINETEEN

Isabelle

Isabelle Elaina Moraco, aka Paige Harper, that was me, alive and well after a near death plane ride. Stuck in a palace by an evil uncle whose only selfish plan was to keep me locked up so that he could inherit the money promised to him for not only bringing me back, but marrying me off to a man I didn't know nor want. I would have given up a million dollars to be with the man that I could see spending the rest of my life with. A man who did things to me that no other man would ever be able to.

Looking out the window into the blue sea, I heard a light tap on my door. Without taking my eyes off of the crystal blue water, I yelled, "Come in."

I could hear the wheels of the service cart as one of the maids of the house began wheeling it in my room. It had been three days that I had been kept in this room. There was always a palace servant at my beck and call, but that didn't matter. All I wanted was to get back to Hawk, where I knew I would be happy. I just didn't know how I was ever going to be able to do that. Focusing my thoughts on Hawk, I heard a soft voice.

"Your dinner is ready, Princess Isabelle. If you would like, I can draw you a bath once you are finished eating," the young girl, who couldn't have been more than eighteen, said.

Turning to face her, I said, "A bath would be nice. I'm not very hungry. Can you please get it ready for me now?"

"Yes, Princess. Right away," she answered, lowering her head and stepping backwards a few steps before she turned to go to the bathroom.

Even though my appetite left the minute we landed

on Kierabali, the food on the cart smelled wonderful. Pushing from the bench in front of the window, I walked over to the cart and lifted the dome off of the plate. Underneath, on the porcelain set in gold plate, was a small Cornish hen seasoned with rosemary and thyme. On the side of the hen were a few sticks of asparagus covered in some sort of sauce. As inviting as it looked, I just couldn't bring myself to eat anything. So instead I poured a good portion of red wine from the decanter into a crystal wine glass and took a seat on the couch. Taking a sip, I waited for the servant to enter the room to let me know that my bath was ready.

Holding a silk red robe, she walked over to where I was sitting and held the robe open while waiting for me to undress. Slipping into the softness of the silk, I took hold of the sash and tied it securely around my waist. Walking towards the bathroom, I remembered my glass of wine that I sat on the small end table while I got undressed. Turning, I could see that the servant had picked up the glass and was now holding it in her hand. Giving her a small smile, I turned and proceeded to the bathroom where I could smell the scent of lavender and vanilla.

exposed of my body.

“I did knock, Isabelle, but you must have been preoccupied,” he replied with a chuckle.

“Get out!” I shouted, throwing the bath sponge in his direction and missing his entire body.

As he left, all I could hear was the annoying yet sexy laugh as he closed the door. If there ever was a more embarrassing moment than this one, it wasn’t on the top of the totally humiliating chart with this. Pulling the plug from the bottom of the large tub. I pushed up with my hands and stepped over the edge. Grabbing the plush, warm towel from the towel warmer, I wrapped it around my body, hoping to cover some of my discomfort from minutes ago. When I was dried off enough. I covered myself with the red robe and tied the sash tightly around my waist. When I opened the door, it didn’t surprise me that Victor was sitting at the table eating the meal that had been prepared for me.

As I stared at him in disbelief, he said with a smile,

"You know, this is really quite good, You should have a bite. Your lack of appetite is beginning to show on your already thin body."

"Why the hell should you even care about what my body looks like? You will never see it, nor touch it, for that matter. Ever." I cursed.

"My, my, aren't we in a mood," he said. "No matter. I'm here to let you know we are going to be making a formal announcement of our plans to marry. Just wanted you to be prepared."

I could have strangled him, but unfortunately I didn't get the chance. He was up and out of his seat before I had a chance to get my hands around his neck. Holding me close, I could feel his breath on my neck as he said with arrogance, "You know, Isabelle, you really should stop fighting this. I will always win."

Before I could say another word, he was at the door. Grabbing the closest thing I could throw at him, I threw the pillow as hard as I could. When it hit him in the back of the head, I jumped for joy inside. It was only after he picked it up and placed it on a small table by the door that I knew I shouldn't have done that. The look he had given me was more evil than any look I got from my uncle. When he left the room with no other word, I fell to the couch and took in a sigh of relief. I knew that I needed to be very careful around Victor Walsh. He was not a man to mess with.

~****~

As my toes extended and my body stretched, I could feel some of the tension I had built up yesterday begin to relax. After my little episode with Victor, my body was knotted with tension and frustration. He had no right to come into my bedroom, let alone stand there and watch me masturbate while in the bathtub. I didn't know who he thought he was, but the fact that he might be the next prince did not give him the right to have control over me.

Pushing from the bed, I grabbed my robe and headed to the bedroom door. Opening it just an inch, I could see that the guard assigned to my room was still standing at full attention. Just like every other day that I had been cooped up in this room. He was there in the morning when I got up and he was there in the evening when I went to bed. Going to the bathroom, there was a green floral dress, matching sling-back heels, and a green hat with lace draped in the front neatly placed on a hanger. Even the clothing was picked out for me. This was going too far. It was one thing to have my husband chosen for me, but my clothes? No way in hell. Grabbing the dress, I walked over to the walk-in closet and hung the dress back up. Rummaging through the dozens of dress and pant suits, I finally found what I was looking for. Tucked away in a corner were a pair of jeans and a faded t-shirt. Even though I had no choice in panties and underwear, at least I still had the clothes that I was most comfortable in hidden away in the back of my closet. My dad used to tell me all the time, I should have been a boy. While girls usually played with dolls and had make-believe tea parties, I was playing in the mud with rocks and fishing off the rocks by the ocean.

Slipping on my jeans and the t-shirt, I had to smile at how comfortable I looked. I also had to chuckle because Victor and my uncle were going to flip out when they saw me wearing jeans instead of the green dress that was laid out for me. I couldn't care less about how I looked when Victor announced his plans for marriage. Matter of fact, I thought I might just make myself scarce during that event. As I was putting my hair back in a pony there was a sharp rap at the door.

Heading towards the annoying sound, I was greeted by my never-to-be husband, "What the hell, Isabelle? We are due to announce our wedding plans in fifteen minutes and you aren't even dressed," he cursed.

"I am dressed, and this is as good as it is going to get," I replied.

I guess I must have said the wrong thing, because before I knew it, Victor's hand came across my cheek, sending a burning sensation all the way around my head to the other side of my face. "You will not defy me, Isabelle. I will always win. You have five minutes to change out of those ridiculous clothes and into something more appropriate."

Just like that, he was gone.

CHAPTER TWENTY

Hawk

After Peter and Sly left, I knew that I needed to start somewhere to find a way to get to Paige. The only place I could think of to look was in her apartment. I was pretty confident that she would have taken a piece of her childhood with her when she fled the country. Locking the door to the motel room, I got in my car and drove the few blocks to her apartment. I hoped that Nikki was there so she could help me find the information I needed to get to Paige.

Rounding the corner of the bar and heading down the alley, I put the car in park and headed up the steps to Paige's apartment. I lightly tapped on the door, hoping that Nikki would be opening it. The minute the door opened, I was thankful that she was still here.

"Hey, Hawk. Any more news on Paige?" she asked.

"Yeah, found out her real name is Isabelle Moraco and she is the princess of Kierabali. Just like you said, she ran away because she was being forced to live a life she didn't want," I replied. "We need to search her apartment to see if we can find out any more information on her. Looks like it is just going to be me and you working together to get her back."

I hated having to bring Nikki into this, but she was the closest person to Paige and knew more about her than anyone else. Walking past her, the first place I began searching was her bedroom, while Nikki began searching the living area. I knew that a bedroom was like a woman's castle. If there was anything to be found, it would be there. Opening the door to her room, I thought about how messy her room was and also how a princess could be so messy. I was no Mr. Clean myself, but she was a pig, though still a very beautiful one. The first place I went was to the small dresser. Pulling open the drawers, there wasn't anything out of the ordinary inside: bras, panties, socks. The basic essentials for a woman. When nothing came up in my search, I decided my next search would be in her closet. It would be great if I could find a shoe box or something filled with the treasures I was looking for. Once again, only clothes and shoes.

These were the two obvious places that a girl would hide stuff. Sitting on the bed, it dawned on me. There was only one other place that Paige would have hidden her past. Rising from the bed, I took hold of the mattress and flipped it off. There it was, the mother-load. Only it really wasn't. Laying on top of the box spring was a manila envelope. Sitting back down on the box spring, I flipped the envelope over and undid the clasp. Shaking the contents onto the bed, I could see that the envelope did indeed hold information about Paige's past. Picking up the first piece of information, I unfolded the documents to find it was actually death certificates on her mom and dad. As I scanned the documents, I couldn't help but wonder how two people in their forties could have died so tragically. Scattering the rest of the papers on the bed so I could see everything, I grabbed a picture of a mangled car. I could only assume that it was the car Paige's parents were driving, which caused their death.

Running my hand through my hair, I could only imagine how horrible it must have been for Paige to lose her parents at such a young age. Taking a closer look at the picture, I noticed that there was something inside the engine that didn't look like it belonged. As mangled as the car was, I knew the components of a car engine like the back of my hand, and this thing, whatever it was, wasn't part of an engine's makeup. Rummaging through the rest of the items from the folder, I came across another interesting piece of information. It was a picture of two men exchanging briefcases. It seemed kind of odd that Paige would have a picture of this among her things. Most of the rest of the stuff really didn't make sense to me. A few pictures and a couple of legal documents. Holding on to the two pictures, I put everything back inside the envelope.

I knew that there was no way that I would be able to do this on my own. My only prayer was that Peter and Sly's flight hadn't taken off yet. Pulling my cell from my pocket, I pulled up Peter's contact info and dialed his number.

“Hawk, If you are calling to talk me into changing my mind, you don’t need to,” Peter stated.

“I think once you hear what I have to say, you will.” I asserted.

“Whatever it is, it can wait. We are on our way back to the motel,” Peter began. “You are my brother, and I can’t just leave you hanging dry. It just took me some time to realize it. Well, that and the help of Sly.”

“Come to Paige’s apartment instead. It is in the back of Hell’s Gate, down the alley. I’ve got something to show you. I think Paige is in more danger than just being taken,” I pointed out.

“On our way, bro.”

I knew that Peter would never leave me to my own devices. We had served together and had been brothers ever since. We always had each other’s back, no matter what. ‘One for all and all for one.’

~****~

It seemed like we had been at it all night piecing together the information I found in the manila envelope. Peter was pretty head smart. He figured out some things that I didn't even see. Like the fact that the death of Paige's mother and father happened a few days after the date and time stamped on the photo with the two men. Also the fact that this Maxwell Moraco was named the trustee for Isabelle in the event something happened to her parents. One thing we couldn't understand was why an investigation into the death of her parents wasn't conducted. It seemed pretty odd since with them being of regal descent; there usually would have been some sort of investigation. Peter seemed to think that it might have something to do with the picture of the briefcase exchange.

No matter, at least now I wouldn't be doing this alone. I had my brothers with me. Calling it a night, we headed back to the motel, leaving Nikki to stay at the apartment. We told her we would be back in touch tomorrow morning and come up with a game plan. As much as I hated getting her involved, she might be our only way into Kierabali. I headed to my room, while Peter and Sly checked in. One thing nice about this town was there weren't too many visitors and rooms were always available.

Settling on the bed, I began going over everything that we had talked about. The only thing I could think about was what Paige was doing this very moment. God, how I wished she was with me right now. Just the thought of her being here beside me made my cock jump to life. Leaning my head against the headboard, I closed my eyes and let my thoughts of Paige take over. It wasn't long until my hand was grasping my hard cock, imagining that it was Paige's soft lips wrapped around it. I could see the movement of her tongue on my cock as she swirled the tip before taking me deeper inside her mouth. The movement of my hand increased as I continued to think of only her. How much I wanted to feel the tightness of her perfect pussy wrapped around my cock, pushing and pulling as her walls tightened around me.

I wasn't one to get off by myself, but to be taken by a woman other Paige was something I could no longer do.

She was everything to me. I wasn't sure what I would do if I ever lost her. "Oh, fucking God, is this what love is? To have your heart hurting so badly?" I shouted as my juices spilled on my stomach. *How could one woman capture my heart to the point that I couldn't fucking think straight?*

Needing to clean up, I pushed from the bed and headed to the shower. Instead of turning on the hot water, I turned on the cold. Anything to help tone down the semi-hard erection that was again on the verge of exploding. The timing of whomever was at the door couldn't have been any worse. Grabbing a towel and wrapping it around my body, I turned off the water and headed to the door. The minute I opened it, I knew I should have ignored it.

"What are you doing here, Erica?" I asked, looking to see if there was anyone else outside, namely Peter and Sly.

"We need to talk, Jayce," she answered.

Tugging on her arm to get her inside, I closed the door. I wasn't sure what she thought she needed to talk about, but I wasn't about to stand in front of the door to find out. "Whatever you need to talk about couldn't have waited until the morning?" I asked.

"No, it couldn't," she began, rubbing her hands up and down her arms as she began pacing the floor. "I want things to be the way they were between us, Do you know how hard it is to find a man that would do the things that you did?"

"We've already talked about this, Erica. What we had is in the past. I've moved on," I replied.

"Well, there is something else you need to know." she said.

"Yeah, there is something I need to know. The little boy. Who is the dad?" I asked, praying he wasn't mine.

"If you are talking about Charlie, he's not yours," she said stopping long enough to explain. "The night before you left, I lied to you. I didn't want you to leave. I stopped taking my birth control pills the day you told me you were leaving Stillwater and you would be gone in a couple of weeks. I knew if I told you, we would have never had that last night together. I wanted something that would remind me of you, but it was too late. I was so angry with you for wanting to leave that I went to Hell's Gate to find comfort. Your brother was there. One thing led to another and we ended up in bed together. Drew is Charles' dad"

"Does he know?" I asked.

"No, I've never told anyone. I wanted to wait until you came back. I was going to lie and tell you that you were his dad, but I couldn't do that to Charlie. He has a right to know who his real dad is when he gets older." she confessed.

"I can't believe this shit. After all this time, you knew and didn't say anything?" I cursed.

"Do you know how hard it's been for me? You left me without even telling me where you would be. I was hanging on a dream for five years that you would come back and help me raise Charlie. We could have been a family," she confessed.

"That's messed up, Erica. You need to tell Drew," I cursed

"I know I do, but I want you, Jayce. I want us to be a family. Charlie and I both need you in our lives."

"That isn't going to happen, Erica. You're a beautiful woman. Drew is a good man, he will take care of you and Charlie." I pointed out.

"He has a family of his own. I don't care about him. I want you," she argued with a crack in her voice.

"I love someone else, Erica," I admitted.

The minute I said those words, something inside me broke, but not in the way one would think. The tension that I was holding all of a sudden disappeared. I finally knew the feeling I had for Paige was more than just caring for her. I truly loved her and I was finally able to admit it to myself. Even though Erica wasn't happy about my confession, it was the truth. By the look on Erica's face, she knew she was defeated and she would never have my love. Just as quickly as she came, she was gone. I tried to go after her, but running after a heartbroken woman with only a towel on wasn't the most ideal situation. This was probably for the best anyway. Hopefully, if I gave her a little space, she would be able to accept what I told her.

CHAPTER TWENTY-ONE

Isabelle

I cursed every word I could think of as soon as Victor left. There was no way in hell that I was going to let him know that the slap he laid across my face really hurt. Walking to the bathroom, I could see a slight bruise was already beginning to form under my eye. Grabbing my compact, I dabbed some makeup on the reddened area and hoped that it wouldn't be too noticeable. One thing I did know was that I didn't like being told what to do and then punished for not doing it. Somehow I needed to find a way off this island.

Taking the dress that was originally set out for me, I slipped it on and pulled the hidden zipper up. Even though it wasn't my choice of color, I had to admit that it did look pretty good on me. Defying him, I choose to wear a more conservative heel instead of the four-inch stilettos that accompanied the dress. As far as the hat, that was definitely a no-go. Instead, I removed the lace from the front and wrapped it around my ponytail to make it look more elegant. Looking at myself in the wardrobe mirror, I had to admit, I looked pretty good. Victor would just have to accept my choice.

I had already planned what I was going to say during the wedding announcement. I was going to tell all the people that I was being forced to marry a man that I didn't love. I was also going to tell them that I wished to give up my crown as Princess of Kierabali and that I was being held on the island against my will. The people might be angry with me, but that was my wish. Taking one last look in the mirror, I heard a knock at the door. Heading in that direction, I opened to door to see the young girl that was assigned as my servant standing outside, holding a tray with a tea pot and a few crumpets.

"Sir Maxwell thought you might want some tea and a snack before your announcement to the people," she said in a soft voice.

Moving aside so that she could pass, I asked with confusion, “I thought I only had five minutes before the announcement ceremony was to begin?”

“Yes, Princess. Sir Victor has postponed it for an hour so that you have more time to relax and prepare for the event,” she advised, setting the tray on the small table and pouring the tea into the cup. “I will leave you to your tea.”

As soon as she was gone, I grabbed the hot tea and took a seat on the couch. The tea tasted of raspberry and honey. It was actually quite good, even though I wasn’t much of a tea person. As I drank the remaining tea, there was another knock on the door. Pushing from the couch, I felt a little lightheaded. I thought it might have been because I stood too quickly. Getting my bearings, I headed to answer the door. Something wasn’t right. My head felt strange. Almost like I had gone on a drinking binge.

Managing to get to the door, I swung it open to find the Victor was on the other side looking absolutely gorgeous. Taking me by the hand, he placed a soft kiss on the back and said, "Are you ready, beautiful?"

With a nod, I replied, "Yes."

I wasn't sure what was going on with me, but it was like I didn't have a care in the world. I would have jumped off a cliff if he had asked me to. With my hand still in his, he led me down the long hallway and down the steps. Maxwell was waiting for us at the bottom, as well as the servants, who were lined up perfectly with the women wearing black dresses and white aprons and the men wearing black suits with white shirts and a black tie. It was very regal, almost like they were waiting for their daily work instructions. As we walked past them, they either bowed or curtsied with their heads lowered. I didn't know what the big fuss was about. You would have thought it was some kind of inauguration or something instead of a wedding announcement.

Walking out the front door to the podium that was waiting for us just inside the gate, I could see thousands of men and women standing on the other side. Victor stepped up to the podium waving his hands in a manner to let the people who were cheering know they needed to silence themselves. Once the people had calmed and they were no longer cheering, he began his speech.

"People of Kierabali, this is a very exciting day for not only me, but for Princess Isabelle. We would like to share this special day with you as we announce our plans to marry." The crowd began cheering again at Victor's announcement. Some of them even began throwing roses through the gate.

"Please, please," Maxwell said, trying to tone down the excitement of the crowd.

"I know that you are all very excited about this wonderful news that we are sharing. The official date of the wedding will be next Saturday. Speaking for the princess as well as myself, you are all invited to witness this wonderful day."

I don't know what was going on with me, I just stood there watching the excitement touch everyone's face as smiles began to appear. Victor took my hand and we turned back to the front door. I could still hear the crowd cheering and singing the anthem of Kierabali as we entered the palace

Closing the door behind us, Maxwell looked down on me and said with concern, “Isabelle, you don’t look very well. Perhaps a little rest before lunch will make you feel better.”

I did feel tired all of a sudden. “I think I will lay down for a bit,” I agreed.

Walking up the steps, the lightheadedness once again returned, only this time twice as bad. My eyes began losing focus and I could feel my body begin to fall. I was thankful that Victor was right there to catch me. Lifting me from the floor, he took me into his arms and carried me up the flight of stairs.

Once we got to my room, he placed me on the bed and covered me with the small blanket that was draped across the foot end. Brushing my cheek with his hand, he leaned over and kissed me tenderly on the lips. “Rest, my princess.” My eyes closed and everything went dark.

~****~

Walking hand in hand on the beach was so surreal. Hawk was the best thing that had ever happened to me. While the warmth of the blue water brushed our bare feet, I knew that this moment was something I wanted to share with him over and over again. Kierabali was a beautiful place, and spending every day here knowing that the man that I loved was here with me, made it that much better. "Hawk, my prince."

Just as the wonderful thoughts of me and Hawk together filled my mind they were taken away. Unsure of what caused my eyes to spring open, my heart dropped as the blue eyes that I remembered the day my father died were staring back at me.

"If you want your friend Hawk to remain alive, you need to forget about him, Isabelle. Your life is with Victor. He is the only man that should be filling your thoughts," he declared.

"I will never love another man," I swore.

"I beg to differ, Isabelle. You will love Victor. And you will be marrying him next Saturday," he vowed. "Now get yourself together. Lunch is in twenty minutes."

Before I could respond, he was gone. My heart felt empty. All I wanted was the one man that I knew I could never be with. If Hawk was to remain safe, I needed to forget about him. That was easier said than done. There was no way I would ever forget about him. I needed to find a way off of this island. Maybe I could ask the people of Kierabali to help me. They needed to know the truth. They needed to know what was going on.

Sliding from the bed, I went to the bathroom to make myself presentable for lunch. As I looked in the mirror, I looked as if I hadn't slept for a week. Come to think of it, it felt like I was off a little. Turning on the cold water, I splashed it on my face, hoping that would help clear my mind. Drying off my face, I could clearly see that I still looked tired.

Giving up on my appearance, I walked over to the door and rushed out before I was punished for not showing up on time. As I walked down the steps, I remembered seeing the servants earlier, but nothing afterwards. I didn't even remember the wedding announcement very clearly, other than hearing the cheering of the crowd. It wasn't like me to only remember bits and pieces. It was almost as if I was drugged. *"Holy mother of God, that had to be it. The tea,"* I thought to myself.

CHAPTER TWENTY-TWO
Hawk

Waking up the next morning was like I had never gone to sleep. My mind must have been going a mile a minute last night just thinking about what needed to be done in order to get to Paige. I hated the fact that we needed to include Nikki in our plan, but she was the only person who would be able to get close enough to Paige so that we could get inside the walls of the palace.

Pulling me from my thoughts, there was a knock at the door. I slid from the bed to see who it might be. Opening the door, Peter and Sly were standing just outside.

"Hey, bro. You look like hell. Did you even sleep?" Peter questioned.

"Good morning to you too," I snapped back.

"We need to get going if we are going to make it to Kierabali by night," Sly commented.

"Let me grab my bag and we can head out," I said.

As I grabbed the remainder of my things, Peter and Sly stayed just outside the door. The minute I closed the door behind me, it finally hit me. "Guys, wait. We need to rethink our plan. How the hell are we going to get Nikki inside the gates of the palace?" I asked with concern.

"You leave that to us. You just concentrate on being with Paige," Peter directed.

As we left the motel, I began sorting out all of the things that could possibly go wrong. This was Paige's life we were talking about. One mistake and we all could be looking at the end of our lives. Before I knew it, we were pulling up to Hell's Gate. Peter refused to sit in the back of my Mustang. Even thought we were about the same size,

Sly would never be able to get back there with his 6’4” frame. So, being the friend that I was, I let Peter drive while I sat in the back.

Nikki was already waiting patiently at the bottom of the steps. Sly exited the car and helped Nikki with her bag. Popping the trunk of the car, he loaded her bag and allowed her to sit in front seat while taking the back with me. Go figure, he wasn’t willing to sit in the back before, but when a woman was involved, he would gladly give up the front seat for her.

Giving him one of my “what the fuck” signature looks, I moved over to allow him to squeeze his large frame into the back seat. It was bad enough for me to be sitting in the back with no room, but to have two big men sitting on a seat that was clearly made for one was less than ideal.

“Let’s get this show on the road,” Peter said, knocking me from my current thoughts.

An hour later we were at the Tulsa International airport. It was the longest and most uncomfortable hour I had ever ridden in a car before. As we pulled up to the long term parking area, it took everything I had to maneuver my body out of the confined space. That was, of course, after I laughed my ass off watching Sly attempt the same task.

Grabbing our things from the trunk, we headed inside the airport to our designated gate. By the time we went through security, we still had an hour to wait. Peter thought it would be a good time to go through the plan again to make sure nothing was left out.

"Okay, so this is how it is going to go down. Nikki, are you set for what you need to do?" Peter questioned.

"As ready as I'll ever be. The agency is expecting me. From there, I am to be taken to the palace to begin my job as Paige's personal servant," Nikki confirmed.

"Good, remember to give Paige the earpiece so that she will know exactly how everything is going to go down. The last thing we need is her uncle to get wind of what is happening." Peter advised.

"Hawk, I know this is going to be hard for you, but you need to stay away from the palace. If they see you, it could blow our plans sky high," Sly cautioned.

"I know what I need to do, Sly. I will lay low. Paige's safety is the most important thing," I pointed out.

~****~

I was thankful that Peter allowed me to sit at the window seat. Not only did I hate flying, other than being the pilot, I hated the aisle seat. Knowing that the flight to Kierabali was eleven hours, about the only thing to do was to lay back and relax. Leaning my seat back as far as it would go, I could only concentrate on the conversation that Sly and Nikki were having behind me. I was glad that they were getting along so well, but it occurred to me that they had nothing in common. Granted, I wasn't sure what Paige and I had in common either. The only thing that mattered was that I was falling for her and wanted to spend the rest of my life with her.

As I looked out the window, the plane began climbing higher and higher. It wasn't long before it reached altitude and the land below us disappeared, and only the white clouds could be seen. It reminded me of the heavens and also how shitty I felt leaving Drew to attend Ma's funeral himself. Saving Paige was all I cared about. Drowning out the noise, I concentrated on my breathing and was finally able to close my eyes and relax.

"Her body is gorgeous," I thought to myself as she laid next to me so peaceful and content. I turned to face her, watching the rise and fall of her perfect breasts with each breath she took. Leaning over, I gently kissed her on the shoulder and then again on her collarbone. Her eyes fluttered open and a smile appeared on her beautiful face. She was an angel dressed in white as the sheet covered her soft skin, exposing only one breast and one leg. Lowering my head further, I traced her perfect nipple with my tongue, before I placed my mouth over the areola and sucked gently on the small yet flawless peak. I loved her scent. The way her body smelled of lavender and vanilla, or maybe it was cherry and almonds. It didn't matter, because whatever it was made me want to taste more of her.

As if she knew exactly what I was thinking, her

arms lifted above her head and her hands gripped the white spirals of her headboard. It was the sexiest thing I had ever seen as her back arched, lifting her breasts higher, allowing me to engulf more of her essence. Working my hands down her silky skin, I placed one hand behind her arched back and the other between her soft legs. The heat escaping from between them, let me know that her body was on fire and ready to be consumed. I dipped first one, then another finger inside her wet channel. With a slight curve of my index finger, I found the sweet spot that drove every woman crazy. Her moans of pleasure filled the air as her back rose even further off the bed..

Pushing up, I placed my body over hers. With my eyes on her, I brushed away a stray hair from her cheek and said softly, “I love you, Paige,” before lowering my lips to hers. Feeling a tug on what I thought was my heart, it was actually my arm. Slapping away the uncomfortable tug so that I could go back to my time with Paige, I realized that I had been dreaming the whole time.

Opening my eyes, I was staring at Peter’s disgruntled stare. “Dude, you got it bad. Damn,” he cursed, rubbing his arm.

"Is everything okay here?" a flight attendant asked as she looked first at Peter and then at me.

"Yes, ma'am, all good," Peter confirmed, sending her a wink and then a gleaming white smile.

I really needed to get it together. My feelings for Paige were getting out of control. Not only did she consume my thoughts when I was awake, she was also there in my dreams. Peter was right, I did have it bad.

CHAPTER TWENTY-THREE

Isabelle

"Isabelle, please open the door," a soft voice said.

I thought that I maybe have been dreaming, but there the voice was again.

"Princess, please, open the door. It's Emily."

Sitting up, I waited for a moment to gather my thoughts. After finally being able to focus on what was taking place, I turned my body and sat on the edge of the bed before standing and walking to the door. Even though the door wasn't locked, the person on the other side was considerate enough to wait until I opened the door.

As I turned the knob, another cry sounded, "Hurry, Princess, hurry."

Opening the door, my personal servant was standing on the other side looking terrified. As she squeezed her body past mine, I quickly poked my head outside the door to make sure no one was in sight. Closing the door, I turned to the young girl, who I just found out was named Emily.

"What is going on, Emily?" I asked with concern.

"Princess, something is very wrong. I have been let go. Come, sit, quickly!" she said, holding her hand out to me.

I wasn't sure what was going on, but whatever it was had her anxious and scared. Taking her hand, I let her lead me over to the couch, where we took a seat.

"Sir Maxwell is a bad man, Princess. I knew something was wrong with the tea they had me bring you. I tried to switch the contents, but unfortunately I was unable to. Sir Victor entered the kitchen just as I was getting ready to pour it out. I had to lie and tell him that I thought I saw something floating inside the pot. When he opened the lid and found nothing, I had no choice but to serve it to you. I wanted to tell you then not to drink it, but I was afraid he would hear me. He was standing outside the door when I brought it in," she confessed.

"Wait, so they did give me something?" I paused, waiting for her to respond, When she nodded, I continued, "Emily, you need to tell me what else is going on. I don't trust either one of them."

"I know, Princess. I don't either. All I know is that it is very important that Victor be married to you by next Saturday. If the wedding doesn't take place by then, I'm sure something bad will happen."

"So why are they letting you go?" I asked, concerned.

"I think because I know too much. They say it is for a vacation, but I know I will not be coming back. They have contacted the agency and a new servant is supposed to be here tomorrow. Please be careful, Princess."

After I let her know that everything would be fine, she left my room, making sure that no one was lurking in the hallway. As the door closed behind her, I wondered about what she said. Why would Victor need to marry me by Saturday? What would happen if he didn't? Would something bad happen to me or to him? I wished that I had the answers to these questions. I just needed to keep my eyes and ears open. Maybe then I would be able to find out exactly what was really going on.

With Emily gone, I began getting ready for the day. Taking a long shower, I was able to really clear my head and begin my own plan in figuring out what the two evils were planning. One thing I did know for sure was that I was done being cooped up in this bedroom. I didn't care what it took, even if it meant being escorted by Tweedle Dee and Tweedle Dum, I was getting out of this prison.

Knowing I needed to be on my best behavior, I became the perfect princess. Dressing the part, I chose to wear a silk floral print dress with a matching sweater and sling back heels. I pulled my hair back in a high ponytail, taking a piece of hair and wrapping it around so that the hair tie was covered. Adding a hint of mascara and light pink lip gloss, I was ready to play the biggest part any producer would be proud of.

As I opened the door, I looked to the right and then to the left, seeing that the coast was clear. Heading down the marble steps, all was quiet, which to me seemed very unusual. Not even the voices of the servants could be heard. When I hit the bottom step, the front door opened. Standing before me was Victor, wearing tan riding pants and leather boots, holding a riding crop in one hand and a helmet in the other. I could feel a small tingle between my legs begin to take hold. As much as I despised this man, he was still very handsome.

Lowing my head to hide my arousal, I heard his boots slap against the marble as his steps towards me became louder. Before I could head in the opposite direction, he reached me and lifted my head so that my eyes met his. “You look absolutely beautiful this morning, Isabelle,” he confessed before his lips touched mine in a tender kiss that sent a bolt of electricity to my core.

When he pulled away from me, my lips were still tingling from the touch of his lips on mine. As my eyes opened, his eyes were on me, knowing the effect his kiss had on me.

With a smile revealing his arrogance, he said, “Breakfast is being served on the patio. You go ahead, I’ll be right there.”

Unable to get a word out. I turned toward the double doors and headed to the patio that overlooked the ocean. The only thing I could remember about this patio was the last time my father and I shared a meal together before he left for his appointment with the family attorney. A man my father trusted, but who I had doubts about.

Opening the doors, the warm sea breeze hit my face, giving me a feeling of comfort as I looked out to the beach, which was just beyond the cliff. The steps leading to the beach, I noticed, had been removed. It was the only way to the ocean front from this side of the palace. It made me wonder why they were gone. So many times I had walked down those steps just to be with my father while he sat close to the shore, waiting for a fish to take the worm that he almost always let me bait the hook of his fishing pole with.

Walking to the edge of the patio, I stepped onto the plush green grass. As my heels dug into the soft ground, I lifted one foot, removing my sling back, and then the other. The feel of the cool grass between my toes brought back yet another memory. It was the many pretend picnics I used to have with the company of my dolls. My father would always make it extra special when he brought out Mom's freshly baked sugar cookies and milk. He used to sit with me on the blanket, kicking off his shoes and removing his socks, just dipping the cookies in the milk and then eating them as the milk dripped on his chin. I used to laugh at him and show him how a pro did it. God, I missed him so much.

Looking over the edge of the cliff, lost in my thoughts, I felt a warm touch on my shoulder and a soft kiss on my neck. Closing my eyes to hide my grief, I wished it was Hawk standing behind me. How I wished my father were still alive. I knew that if he was, he would absolutely love Hawk.

"What has you so lost in thought, precious?" Victor asked, wrapping his arms around my waist.

Pulling away from him, I wiped away the tear I felt escaped and answered, "Nothing. What happened to the stairs leading down to the beach?"

"Your uncle had them removed. Felt it was too dangerous having them. Just another way for unwanted guests to have access to the palace." Victor replied.

"Or prevent someone from escaping," I added.

As I walked away from the edge, I heard his stern voice, "Isabelle."

Stopping, I stood there still facing the patio. "Yes."

"Whatever you are thinking, you will never defeat me. You are mine, whether you like it or not."

The minute those words left his lips, my stomach began to bind, sending the bile up my throat. It took everything I had not to lose it all. Clenching my hands into tight fists, I walked up the few steps to the patio and then through the double doors. I could hear Victor behind me calling my name. There was no way he was ever going to have me or that I would ever be his. There was only one man that I belonged to. I knew in my heart that he was coming for me. I just hoped he would get to me soon, before it was too late.

Reaching for the handle of the door, I felt a tight grip on my arm. Before I could pull away from him, Victor's mouth was on mine. The force of his tongue separated my lips, causing them to open and allowing him access to my mouth. Anger began to flare and it was his bottom lip that got the wrath of my fury as I bit down. It was the wrong thing to do, because no sooner had he pulled away and the blood began to show, his hand came across my cheek. My head was swimming from the impact and the jolt of my body being swung over his shoulder didn't hit me until his hand came down on my ass.

"You will learn to respect me, Isabelle. And as you are mine, you will learn to obey me," he cursed.

As I hit him with everything I had, he continued holding tightly onto my body. The anger and disgust I had for this man only added more fuel to the fire that was already burning inside. "Put me down, Victor!" I shouted, hoping that everyone in the palace would hear.

"You can yell and scream all you want, my pet. No one can hear you. It is only us here," he confessed with an arrogant laugh. "For once and for all, you are going to learn who owns you."

I didn't stop hitting him, even though I could feel exhaustion take hold. I was not going to let this man win. It was only after we began descending the steps to the basement of the palace that my efforts stopped. "Where are you taking me, Victor?"

"A place where you will learn your lesson," he answered.

I could feel the coolness of the basement on my body the lower we got. I remembered when I was young I always wanted to know what was beyond the door in the kitchen that always remained locked. When I asked my father about it, he told me it was where evil dwells. I never asked him again, fearing that if I did, it would be coming after me. I later learned that in the late 1800's it was used as a torture chamber for unwanted trespassers. It was used to gain information. Now I would finally know what evil really was.

CHAPTER TWENTY-FOUR

Hawk

I couldn't have been happier when the pilot announced that we would be descending shortly and landing at the Kierabali airport. The island itself wasn't very large. Finding out that Paige was actually a princess made me want to know everything there was to know about this small country. Like the fact that even thought her mother and father were no longer living and they were in fact the King and Queen of Kierabali, Paige would remain the Princess of Kierabali until she was able to bear a child that she could hand down the title of Prince or Princess too. I also learned that in order for Paige to be handed the command of the county she would need to marry the man that was chosen for her at birth, and the marriage needed to take place on the day on which the small country was founded, which unfortunately for us, was five days away.

If we were going to get Paige off that island, we needed to hurry, otherwise our efforts would have been for nothing. Five days wasn't a lot of time, but Nikki had to earn the trust of Paige's uncle and Victor if this plan was going to work at all. Feeling the landing gear lower, I looked out the window to see the small country come into view. The runway was lined with palm trees that were slightly swaying with the light breeze blowing off the water. Coasting to the terminal gate, the airport transportation team was already in route to unload the luggage from the belly of the airplane onto the luggage carts.

When the airplane came to a complete stop the passengers were already up and about collecting the small bags that were stored in the overhead bins. This was something that I couldn't understand. Instead of waiting, people would much rather grab their belongings when there was little to no room to move. Myself, I preferred to wait until everyone in front cleared out before tackling that job.

When we finally got through customs and out of the airport, reality finally settled in. I was here to save the love of my life. The woman that I wanted to spend the rest of my life with. My heart sank into my stomach when a cab pulled up to the curb displaying an ad on the roof. It was my Paige in the arms of the man I didn't really know but despised. I knew there was something about him that I didn't like or trust when I saw him the first time at Hell's Gate. If I had to guess, he and Paige's uncle were working together to get her here. As I looked at the ad, I could see a somber look in her eyes. It was then that I knew we needed to find her quickly and get her out of this country.

Feeling a tug on my arm. I looked over to see Peter beside me. "Don't overthink this, Hawk. It is only an ad, and you of all people know that anything can be done to those things to make them hide the true picture."

I knew Peter was right. A little photoshopping here and there could make anything look the way they wanted. Taking my eyes off the photo, I climbed into the back seat of the cab with Peter and Nikki while Sly sat up front with the driver. With an island accent the driver asked. "Where to?"

We had reservations at the Rue. It was a little more upscale than what we were typically used to, but given the fact the wedding between Isabelle Moraco and Victor Walsh was the biggest event of the year, there wasn't much left of accommodations. At three hundred dollars a night, which equated to two hundred and sixty-six dollars in Kierabali money, it was our only choice.

Heading away from the airport, the horns from other drivers began honking, letting everyone know to move out of the way. This actually was no different than the cab drivers in New York. Everyone was always in such a hurry to get somewhere. Finally out of the airport on our way to the hotel, it couldn't have come at a better time. We had just escaped the ten-car pileup at the pickup area of the airport. I guess that is what happens when people get impatient.

~****~

After unpacking what little clothing I had, I decide

to head down to the lounge for a much needed drink. Stepping on the elevator, an older lady holding a white poodle occupied the car. She looked to be in her sixties, with the darkest red lipstick I had ever seen. Her hair was just as white as her dog's, with a pink bow clipped on the side of her head. I guess it is really true what people say, that owners really do look like their pets. When the elevator stopped at the lobby floor, I let the elderly lady exit first and proceeded to the hotel bar. Even though it was early afternoon, there were quite a few people inside chatting and enjoying an early afternoon toddy. Sitting at the bar, I ordered my signature JD with a beer chaser.

Turning in my chair while I waited for my drink, I could see that the majority of the people were sitting outside enjoying the warm weather. Something must have sparked their attention because all of a sudden they all stood and walked over to the balcony and began snapping pictures. Needing to know what all the commotion was, I headed in that direction after downing my shot of Jack. Trying to peer over the crowd of people, I was finally able to see what had their attention. Looking in the near distance, my heart just about sank as I watched a man carrying a woman potato sack style through a set of double doors.

"What do you think he is doing with Princess Isabelle?" I heard one woman ask.

"I'm not sure. Maybe they are going to have a romp in the hay," another woman replied with a giggle.

My body had never felt so much tension. It was Paige that they were talking about. Only I didn't see what they did. I saw a man forcing a woman to go with him and the woman trying to get away from him. Paige's hands were flying every which way, hitting whoever was manhandling her. Just as he turned to close the door, I could see that it was the guy from the bar. Looking onward, I finally asked, "Who is the man carrying the princess?"

"That is Victor Walsh. He is going to be the new prince," a man replied, taking another picture of the couple.

"Over my dead body," I cursed.

I may have overstepped my bounds a little with that comment because everyone who was looking over to the palace had their eyes on me. Putting my hands in a surrender position, I said, “Just kidding. You guys really need to loosen up.”

That was a little bit too close to being a disaster. The last thing I needed was to be thrown in jail for confessing to a possible murder. Backing away from the balcony. I headed back inside to finish my beer in peace. As I sat there, Sly and Nikki showed up and took a seat beside me. Downing the last of my beer, I ordered another round, getting Nikki a tequila and Sly a beer.

Looking down at my empty glass, I confessed, “We need to jump on our plan as soon as possible.”

“What’s the rush, bro?” Sly asked, leaning forward.

“You see those people out there,” I began pointing at the looky-loos, who were still taking pictures. “They’re watching the princess being manhandled. Something tells me she is in more danger than we initially thought.”

Sly rose to his feet to see for himself what was going on, while Nikki stayed in her seat. When he came back, he took his seat. "Whoever they were looking at is gone."

"Well, I don't care what you think. She is in danger and I'm not going to sit and watch her get hurt," I replied.

"Hawk, you need to focus, bro. You can't just go over there like some delivery guy and expect them to just let you take her. Let us handle this," Sly demanded.

I knew he was right. I couldn't just walk over there and expect them to just let me inside the gate. The plan we had laid out was good. Even if something went wrong, we had all our bases covered in the event it did. I just needed to be patient and wait one more day. One more day and Paige would be here with me. Once more day and she would be mine.

Pushing from the bar, I needed some air, but mostly I needed to get my head straight. I couldn't let my feelings for Paige get in the way of my judgment. I needed Peter, Nikki, and Sly to handle this. Just like everything else, the hardest part of this whole thing was waiting.

~****~

After I took the time to cool off, I headed back to the hotel to get some much needed sleep. As much as the walk did me good, it also made me think about Paige and what Victor would be doing to her. Taking the elevator to the twentieth floor, I watched the LED panel light up, displaying the passing floors. When it finally stopped on the twentieth floor, I got out and headed to my room. With my room facing the ocean, I could see the palace from my terrace. Opening the sliding glass door, I leaned my upper body over the railing and just watched for any movement. I wished there was a way that I could get closer to see what was really going on over there. Realizing then what I needed to do, I went to the closet, switched out my white t-shirt for a black one, grabbed my combat jacket, and headed out. I was tired of waiting. I needed Paige now. I could no longer wait.

Locking the door to my room, I pressed the down button on the panel and waited for the elevator to arrive. Instead of getting off on the lobby floor, I punched the third floor, where I eventually got off. Taking the stairs was the only way that I could ensure that Peter, Sly, and Nikki wouldn't see me. Instead of opening the door to the lobby, I headed down the small hallway and exited through the employee door and into the kitchen area, where I was able to get to the back door unnoticed. It was a good walk to the palace from the hotel, so when I spotted a bicycle leaning against the stucco building, I checked to see that it wasn't locked with a chain. Pushing it down the alley, I watched as Peter, Sly, and Nikki left in the small rental. I hopped on the bike as soon as I rounded the corner and headed in the direction of the palace. All I could think about was saving Paige and how angry Peter would be if he knew what I was doing.

As long as I kept out of sight, there would be no interference with Peter's plan. I would stay so well hidden that even he wouldn't be able to find me. Riding down the cobblestoned street, I wondered how people actually survived on these things. The road was so bumpy, I knew that my ass was going to be sore by the time I got there. It was still light out, with a few more hours of daylight left before I would be able to make my move.

Once I reached the palace, I hid the bike and myself behind some tall shrubs and waited for it to get dark enough that I could enter without being noticed. The sun began to set and the air was beginning to get cooler. Rising to my feet, I positioned the bike closer to the wall so that I could use it as a ladder to get over the brick fence. Stepping on the seat, I reached up, placing my hand along the edge of the brick wall and hoisted myself up. Stopping to take a look to make sure there were no guards manning the grounds, I slowly lowered myself down the other side. Keeping my body flush against the wall, I saw a huge cluster of trees and bushes among the landscaping. This is where I thought would be the best place to bunker down for the night. Crawling low to the ground, I slithered over to the greenery until my body was safely hidden away under a flowering bush. Taking a deep breath, I looked up to the sky and thanked God that I had made it that far.

CHAPTER TWENTY-FIVE

Isabelle

The smell of the basement was musty and damp. I had no idea what was in store for me, but I knew whatever it was wouldn't be good. Victor only walked a short distance from where the stairs were. Holding onto me with one hand, he reached inside the front pocket of his riding pants and pulled out a key. As I heard the lock turn, I knew this was by far the worst day of my life. Victor pushed the door open and a cool breeze hit the underside of my dress. Closing the door, he placed me on my feet, taking hold of my arms, which were so sore from trying to hit him that I didn't have the strength to pull away.

"Now you will know what it means to obey me, my sweet princess. No more will I be defied," he said, tugging my body closer to him.

His hands worked so quickly that I didn't realize until it was too late that he had slapped a pair of handcuffs on my wrists, binding them in front of me. I tried to free my hands, but it was no use. The harder I tried, the tighter they became. As he backed me up further, to the middle of the room, the dim light made it hard to see my surroundings. He took my handcuffed wrists and snapped on a clasp with a heavy chain attached to it. When he threw it up in the air, I thought for sure that it would come down and get me right between the eyes, but instead it dangled across a pole that was anchored to the ceiling. Taking the end of the chain, Victor began pulling on it, making my arms lift high above my head. I could hear the sound of metal against metal as he continued pulling. When my feet barely hit the cement floor, he finally stopped. I was completely at his mercy.

He stepped away from me, but only long enough to grab something from inside a cabinet that was up against the wall. When he came back, he was holding a knife with a blade that had to have been at least nine inches long. Pressing the tip of the blade against his index finger, he looked up at me with a shit-eating grin. “This will only take a minute. You will need to hold still. I wouldn’t want to mark that beautiful body of yours.”

I had no idea what he was talking about, but he soon clarified my curiosity. He glided the blade under the strap on my shoulder, turned it upward and lifted it, cutting the material like butter. There was nothing that I could do to stop him. I just watched as the material fell. He did the same thing to the other side, causing the dress to fall far enough to expose the strapless bra I was wearing underneath.

“What do you want, Victor?” I asked with a shaky breath.

“To make sure you understand that you are mine,” he said, placing the blade of the knife under the lace of the bra, right between my breasts.

“Please don’t do this, I will do whatever you want,” I pleaded.

"Yes, you will, my pet, but first you will need to learn never to defy me again." Just like that, the blade cut through the lace and my bra fell to the floor, exposing my breasts. My nipples were hard and standing taut for him. Not because of the coldness in the room, but because my body was beginning to feel the onset of anxiety or emotional arousal, which had to have been caused by the fear that was consuming my body at this very moment. I couldn't let him know that I was afraid. Just then I remembered what my dad had told me. "*Whenever you get scared, take your mind to a happy place. A place that makes you feel safe.*" Closing my eyes, I thought about the one place that made me happy.

No sooner than my happy place entered my mind it was gone. Victor tore my dress from my body, leaving me only wearing my lacy black underwear. My eyes snapped open to find that he no longer was holding the knife, but a riding crop. The short distance between us lessened to mere inches. I could feel his breath on my skin as he closed in on me. Sliding the back of his hand down my arm and then down my side, the tingling sensation of his touch caused my body to react in a way I was unable to control. His mouth found mine, forcing me to cease my resistance and give him access. I knew not to fight him. Fighting him was what landed me in this mess in the first place.

"Your body will know what it means to be thoroughly fucked, Princess. When I get done with you, you will know who owns you," Victor whispered between kisses.

Breaking his contact, my eyes opened to find him stepping away and walking behind me. With a flick of the riding crop, I felt a slight sting on my lower back as a small whimper escaped from my mouth. "How many lashings should my pet receive?" he asked, taking the tip of the riding crop and barely touching my body with it.

I wasn't sure what he wanted me to say, but when I didn't answer, another strike hit my back, only this one was a little harder. Coming up with a number, I cried out, "Ten."

"Ten it is, then," he agreed.

One after the other, the pain became more intense as each swing of the crop landed on my back. I was thankful when the tenth one landed. I knew that my back would have red welts from the thin piece of leather. Without so much as a warning, his hand cupped my sex. I let out a small yelp, afraid of what he might find.

"Just as I thought, my little pet likes punishment," he announced

I knew I was wet, but was no longer any attraction to this man. Even though my body said otherwise, I hated this man with everything inside me. I wanted to die, knowing I couldn't control the reaction my body was having. It was only after he slipped his finger under my soaked panties and inside my pussy that he got what he wanted, my submission.

~****~

Every muscle in my body ached. The last thing I remembered was surrendering to my release and then blacking out. Victor must have brought me back to my room and dressed me in the nightgown I was currently wearing. Pushing to a sitting position, I could see that the sun was getting ready to set. It had to be late in the evening. Throwing off the covers, I turned my body and got out of the bed. As soon as I got to the bathroom, I turned on the light and lifted the nightgown over my head. Turning slightly, I needed to see what damage was done to my back. I was surprised to find that there were no welts on my back. The only thing I could see were faint red marks across the lower part. As bad as the strikes hurt, I just couldn't believe that there wasn't any more evidence of Victor's assault. Turning on the water, I splashed some on my face to clean up some of the mess my makeup made. My eyes looked like a raccoon and my cheeks were streaked with black from the tears I promised I wouldn't shed for Victor.

As I was finishing up in the bathroom, there was a tap at the door. Putting my nightgown back on, I turned off the light and went to go answer it. Opening the door, another young servant was standing outside holding a tray. The minute the aroma hit my nose, my stomach began to signal that it was hungry. There was something strange about this servant. Her head was kept low. Moving to the side to let her in, I asked, "What is your name, my name is Pai… I mean Isabelle."

She still didn't answer me. Touching her arm gently to get her attention, she looked up at me. It was then I knew she wasn't able to speak. Her hand went to her throat and her head nodded back and forth. It was the universal sign that she couldn't talk. It made me wonder how awful it would be unable to speak.

As she placed the tray on the small table, I turned and grabbed the robe that was lying on the end of the bed. Before I could thank her she was out the door. Walking over to the small table, I lifted the dome from the plate and looked at the contents. Lifting the plate with both hands, I brought it to my nose to smell the food. It smelled divine and my stomach was ready to devour it. Setting the tray back down on the tray. I lifted the pitcher to pour myself a glass of water. It was then that I remembered what happened the last time I drank something. Placing the pitcher back on the tray, I took the glass and headed to the bathroom where I could fill the glass directly from the tap.

Sitting in silence, I began to consume my meal, which consisted of grilled chicken on a bed of wild rice, steamed zucchini, and mushrooms. No sooner than I got the first bite down, I could feel it coming up. Rushing the bathroom, all of the contents in my stomach spilled. The events from earlier began racing in my head. Now more than ever I needed to find a way off this island. There was no way in hell I would ever marry a man like Victor. The whole reason I left Kierabali was to gain my freedom. The bile in my throat rose again, spilling another round of contents from my stomach. I couldn't let this man get to me, or what he had done, either. Pushing from a kneeling position to my feet, I walked over to the sink and splashed cold water on my face. Straightening my back, I said to myself, "You can do this, Isabelle. You need to be strong."

Crawling into bed, I closed my eyes and did what my father always told me. I found my happy place. And right now, my happy place was Hawk. I had to just keep believing that he would find me. He would be the one to take me in his arms and keep me safe. He would be the one who would be holding me at night while making passionate love to me. Rolling over on my side, I grabbed the pillow next to me and held it tight, and let the tears flow. Everything inside me must have emptied. My eyes fell shut and the darkness entered.

CHAPTER TWENTY-SIX

Hawk

Laying under this bush made me rethink what I was doing. I had insisted on going with Sly to drop Nikki off at the agency that hires the servants for the palace, but Peter ordered me to stay behind. As soon as Peter, Sly, and Nikki got into the small rental car, I knew it was my chance to execute my own plan. I knew the three of them would be able to handle Nikki's part of it. We had already managed to get Nikki registered as an employee at agency with no problem. Thanks to Chavez's computer expertise, something he learned while serving, he was able to hack into the agency's computer system and switch the name of the servant who was going to be assigned to Paige. We weren't sure what was going on with the current servant, other than she was taking an extended leave. It really didn't matter to us. The only thing that matter was the timing couldn't have been more perfect and it was our way into the palace.

When I left the hotel, I figured I'd have about an hour to get to the palace before Nikki even left the agency. The plan was for Peter and Sly to wait until Nikki gave the signal that everything was going as planned. They would wait down the block from the agency, out of sight. With Nikki's earpiece in place they would be able to communicate with her and know when she would be in route to the palace.

I hated playing the waiting game. That was why as soon as the three of them were out of sight, I made my move. So here I was, laying under a damn bush doing something I hated doing, waiting. Adjusting my position so I could at least see what was going on around me, I saw a white van pull up to the gate. I couldn't see who was inside, but with a logo on the side of the van showing a black silhouette of a maid and a butler, I knew Nikki had to be in the van.

Stopping in front of the house, the driver and Nikki exited the van. They were soon at the front door, where another servant appeared. I couldn't tell what they were saying, but I was pretty sure they were exchanging introductions. With Nikki now inside and the driver driving away, I knew that it was only a matter of time until she would be getting to Paige. It was barely getting dark and I knew I had least another hour before it would be dark enough to make my move. The only thing I could do was lay back and wait.

Seeing the stars through the leaves of the bush let me know that the time was near. Rolling over on my stomach, I pulled the small binoculars out of my cargo vest to see if I could see any movement. All I could think about was Paige's reaction when she saw Nikki, or if she would even see her yet tonight. As I looked around, the only thing I could see was basically nothing. The curtains on the windows were pulled closed and most of the light coming from the palace was so dim that it was impossible to see what was going on inside. I needed to get closer. I knew the layout of the palace inside and out; at least, that is, of the map used when renovations were done over a decade ago.

Peter was pretty confident that nothing would have changed during the renovations. It was an historical landmark, so changing the design wouldn't be very profitable. I only hoped that the hidden door was still there.

With no guards milling about outside, my guess was that they were securing the inside, making sure no one got close to Paige. Against my better judgment, I needed to get out from under this bush. My best bet would be to get to the other side of the palace and find the door leading to the basement. I knew that it was hidden on the side, I just had to figure out where. Crawling combat style, I made my way to the brick fence. I knew that if I buddied my body flat against it, I would be able to get to the back side of the palace unseen.

Reaching the back of the palace, I took in my surroundings to make sure there were no guards lurking around. Pulling my night vision glasses from my vest, I tried to find the door I was searching for. Having a pretty good idea where it was, I hurried across the grass to the side of the palace. I could hear some chattering coming from the back. I knew that if whoever was talking came around the side, they would see me. Holding my breath, I lowered my body to the ground and hoped the two men talking wouldn't spot me this low. Just as I feared, they walked to the edge of the patio. Looking up at them, they were thankfully facing the opposite direction. Both of them were smoking. I could only hear bits and pieces of what they were saying as they were too far away. The minute they said Isabelle's name, my hearing got better.

I couldn't stand what they were saying. I had to bite my tongue in order not to cuss at them for their disgusting conversation about what they would do if they ever became her prince. Wanting to hit something, I noticed a small lever hidden behind a rose bush. That had to be the way into the palace. While I was waiting and watching, the two men threw down their cigarette butts and head back the other way. When they were out of sight, I lifted the lever and waited for something to happen. There was nothing, no magic door, nothing. I lifted the lever again. It was then that I noticed the rose bush was moving. *"What the fuck?"* I thought to myself. Sitting on my haunches, I felt around the bush to find there was a gap between the ground and where the bush was planted.

Reaching under the gap, I worked my fingers inside until I had a good grip on what I believed to be a door. As I looked down, I could see there was a set of stairs leading down. I wasn't sure how many there were since I could only see the first three steps. Lifting the door higher, I wiggled my body inside. I needed to be careful not to make a sound. I wasn't sure where the two guards were and the last thing I wanted was for them to find me.

The minute I closed the hidden door, I grabbed my small flashlight and switched it on. Pointing the light down the steps, I could see there were about a dozen steps to the bottom. Sliding my butt down each step, I was finally able to stand on the seventh step down. When I got to the bottom there were different passages. I wasn't sure which one to take. I pulled the map from my pocket and unfolded it. Looking at the layout, it was evident that I was at the northwest side of the palace. It was only a matter of using common sense to know which way I needed to go. Taking a right, I headed down the narrow passageway, hoping that I would come upon a set of stairs leading to the main floor.

I was getting nowhere. It seemed like I was going in circles down here. Pulling the map out again, I took another look at it. It was only then that I figured out why I couldn't find the stairs. They weren't in plain sight. Just like the entrance outside, they had to be hidden behind one of those doors. Beginning where I stood, I started opening the doors to the rooms. Each door I opened was like stepping back in time. It made me glad that torture wasn't used in the States for criminal punishment. If you were guilty of a crime, you just went to jail. Some of the instruments in these rooms I had only read about. I had no idea that they actually existed. There were torturing devices ranging from a guillotine-looking device to a bed with pulley-like levers on each side. Then there were items that I had no idea what they were used for.

When I finally opened the door I was looking for, I was more than ready to get out of this medieval dungeon. Taking the steps slowly, one at a time, I headed up to the main floor. Just before I reached the top, I decided I needed to think about what I was going to do. I didn't even know who might be waiting for me on the other side. Trying to figure out my next move, I remembered the earpiece I stuffed in my pocket before I left the hotel. Placing it in my ear, I tapped to audio and waited for a sound. I knew by activating the earpiece that not only would Nikki hear me, but Peter and Sly would too. I probably wouldn't have a job when I got back to the States, but at least Paige would be with me. There was no way I was leaving here without her.

"Nikki, can you hear me?" I asked. When there was no response, I asked again, "Nikki, are you there?"

"Hawk, is that you?" she asked. It was the sweetest sound I had ever heard.

"Yeah. Where are you?" I replied.

"Where are you? The guys have been going crazy. They think you took off for the palace. Please tell me that you aren't here."

"Yeah, well, I can't. I'm in the palace. In the basement. I need your help. I'm not sure what is on the other side of the door."

"Where do you think you are?"

"I think I might be under the kitchen. Where are you?"

"I'm in the kitchen. It's just me in here."

"Okay, I'm opening the door."

As soon as I pulled on the door, I could see that it was actually the backside of a cupboard. There were shelves loaded with canned goods, which were attached to the door. Squeezing through the small space, I pushed open the door to the cupboard. Adjusting my eyes to the light, I could see that Nikki was standing with her arms crossed in front of another door. She was so focused on waiting for the door to open that she must not have heard me.

Tapping the audio on my earpiece, I whispered, "Nikki, the door you're staring at isn't going to open."

Just then she turned around, showing me a pissed off look. I wasn't sure if it was because I didn't come through that particular door or because I shouldn't have been there in the first place.

"Hawk, are you crazy nuts? You shouldn't be here," she said in a low voice.

"I already know that, Nikki. I just couldn't sit around with my finger up my ass waiting to see what would happen," I remarked.

Pulling me away from the kitchen door, she whispered, "What are you going to do?"

"For now, I'm going to stay out of sight. Have you seen or talked to Paige?"

"No, not yet. The head butler was showing me around and letting me know what my duties will be. I do know that they have her upstairs. There are two big men standing outside her door. I'm guessing either to keep her in or to make sure no one gets to her."

"So why are you in the kitchen?" I asked, confused.

"I was just getting a drink of water before I went to bed. They expect me to be up at 4:00 a.m. to start my duties for the princess," Nikki answered, looking out the swinging door to the dinning area. "We need to get you out of here. You can stay in my room until we can figure out what to do."

For someone who had never done this before, she was pretty smart. Walking close behind her, I followed her lead. The servant's quarters were on the other side of the palace. The risk of us getting caught just doubled. Making our way past the huge dining area and down the long hallway, it surprised me that there was no one around. Pulling on the sleeve of Nikki's uniform to get her attention, I asked quietly, "Where is everyone?"

With her finger to her lips, she said, "They have either turned in or are doing their hourly rounds of the grounds. We should be safe, but we need to hurry."

Just as I said, for someone who had never done this before she was good.

CHAPTER TWENTY-SEVEN

Isabelle

I wasn't sure what was going on with me, but my body hurt and I felt like I never went to sleep. The only thing I could think of that was different was the dinner that I couldn't eat. Rolling over, I hoped that a shower would make me feel better. When I got to the bathroom, there was a knock on the door. Leaning against the counter, I concentrated on my face, noticing how pale it looked. They way I looked was definitely a clue as to how I felt, which was like shit. With the knocking still happening at the door, I decided I better answer it in case it was Victor. The last thing my body could endure right now was more punishment.

Barely able to move, I slowly went to answer the

door. As soon I opened the door, I lost my breath. Not because it was Victor, but because it was the last person I expected to see. “Nikki,” I cried with joy.

“Don’t just stand there, silly. Let me in,” she said calmly.

As soon as I closed the door, I pulled her in for a hug. I had never been so happy in my life. The tears began to fall with so much emotion that my cry of happiness turned into a downpour. When I was finally able to contain myself, I let go of the suffocating hug I was giving her. Only then did it occur to me that she could be putting herself in danger by being here. “Nikki, are you crazy? Do you know what will happen to you if they find out you are here?”

“That’s why you can’t keep calling me Nikki. My name is Abby,” she said.

“Abby, right. Nice wig, by the way,” I said, taking a piece of the blonde hair between my fingers. “What are you doing here?”

“We came to get you out of this hellhole,” she confessed.

“We?” I questioned.

“Yeah, Yours truly, Peter, Sly. And of course your dumb-fuck boyfriend Hawk,” she said sarcastically.

“Wait, did you just say Hawk?” I asked excitedly.

“Yeah. He actually was supposed to stay away, but his hormones got in the way. He’s been a total mess since we got here.”

I knew I needed to tame down my excitement. He didn’t forget about me. Somehow I knew deep down inside he would be coming for me. I pulled Nikki down on the couch to find out what the plan was. It took all of fifteen minutes for her to explain. I went through the instructions again with her. It was a good plan, I just hoped that it would work.

After Nikki left my room, I began thinking about everything that could possibly go wrong. In a way, getting me off this island wasn't different than when I left the first time. I was just glad that I had some help this time. I was a worry wart, though. I was afraid that as much as I wanted their help, it would ultimately cost them their lives.

Still feeling like I could throw up any minute, I knew I needed to try and get something down. The only thing that looked appealing to me was the toast. Taking a small bite, I waited for a moment before taking another. It seemed as though I was able to keep it down. Before long, I had finished one slice of toast and one slice of bacon without feeling sick to my stomach. Covering the remaining food on my plate with a napkin, I headed back to the bathroom for a much needed shower. All I could think about was the fact that in twenty-four hours I would be off of this island and on my way back to the States. I wasn't sure how they found me, but with only three days left until the wedding, I was beginning to get worried that I was never going to leave.

~****~

As I walked down the marble steps, I could hear chatter between the servants. With only three days left, the palace was becoming quite busy. If they only knew that the wedding would be taking place without the bride. I wished I would be able to see the look on Victor's face when he found out that I was no longer on the island. I had to hand it the Kierabali traditions. The groom to be couldn't see the bride three days before the wedding. Everything about Peter's plan was perfect, down to Victor being nowhere near the palace grounds.

Heading to the double doors that lead out to the back patio, I could see that Nikki was already fitting into her new role. She was assisting another servant with a white tablecloth for the dinning room table. As I passed by her, I could see the small smile on her face as she tried to hide it from the other woman. I couldn't help but smile myself.

The first phase of the plan was to get me away from the palace. This wasn't going to be difficult, considering the seamstress for my wedding dress fitting somehow ended up with a small case of food poisoning, which consequently made it possible for me to go to town for the fitting instead. I also knew that the chauffeur that would be driving the car was going to be Peter. Little did my uncle know that my so-called fitting was for something other than a wedding dress. It was for a disguise. In order for me to escape the palace, my uncle and everyone else had to think I was someone else.

I still had a few hours to kill, so I thought the fresh air would do me good. Opening the patio door, there were about a dozen men outside getting the backyard ready for the big event. From what I overheard, the entire ceremony was to be televised. Typically we would have been married in the church, but according to my uncle's statement to the press, it was for security purposed that the venue for the wedding had to be changed. Security, my ass. The change was so they could keep an eye on me to make sure that the wedding happened.

As I was thinking about one day having a real wedding and marrying a man that I really love, there was a slight tap on my shoulder. Turning my body, it was a bigger man in blue overalls and a blue cap. When he raised his head, my heart sank. Hawk put his finger to his lips, signaling for me not to say anything. Taking my hand, he led me to the side of the palace near a cluster of trees. It took everything I had to contain myself. When we were far enough away and out of sight from the other men, he pulled me close and placed his lips on mine. My heart was beating so fast, I thought it was going to burst out of my chest.

When our kiss finally broke, he whispered to me, "I had to see you. I needed to know that you were okay."

"I knew you would come for me. I just knew you would," I said as tears began forming in my eyes.

"Shh, it's okay, baby. I love you, Paige. I would die before I would let them take you from me," Hawk confessed.

"About that, Hawk. I should have been honest with you. My real name is Isabelle."

"I don't care about that. To me, you will always be

Paige. You need to get back before they start looking for you. Soon you will be out of here. Are you ready for the plan?"

"Yeah,"

"Good. I gotta go."

With one final kiss, Hawk walked to the front of the palace, while I headed to the back. There were so many things that I wanted to tell him, but didn't have the chance. As I rounded the corner, Victor was standing on the edge of the patio scanning the area like he was ready to kill something or someone. Just as I stepped up the two steps, he grabbed my arm and pulled me near him. The hold he had on my arm became tighter. Lowering his head to my ear, he whispered in a sharp tone, "I would suggest you stay where I can see you, unless you want more of what you got yesterday, Princess."

I dared not pull away from him. When he kissed me on the forehead, it was all I could do not to pull away from him. Heading inside the palace, Nikki and the other servant girl were already gone. As I walked past the dining table I thought about what Hawk said. He told me that he loved me, but what he didn't know was that I loved him too.

~****~

The ride to the bridal shop was uneventful. There was so much that I wanted to say to Peter, but couldn't. With Victor sitting to my right and my uncle sitting to my left, it was best that I sat in silence. When we pulled up to the bridal shop, I was thankful that I didn't have to endure their company a minute longer. Just when I thought I was clear of them, Victor pulled on my wrist, causing me to lose my footing and end up on his lap. Taking advantage of the situation, he lowered his mouth to mine and kissed me. Not only was it uncomfortable, the kiss was nothing more than his way of showing his control over me.

"We will be back in a couple of hours. Be ready, Isabelle," Uncle Maxwell cautioned.

Without so much as a look at him, I nodded my head and exited the car. Peter was already standing at my the door to assist me. At least there was one gentleman in this group. Peter closed the door and stood outside the car until I entered the shop. Looking his way, he nodded his head, letting me know that everything was ready for me inside.

Stepping inside, a receptionist greeted me and directed me to the back of the shop. She opened a set of wooden doors and instructed to me to have a seat and that someone would be with me shortly. As I took a seat, I began wondering what I would be disguised as. I knew they had it all figured out, but it would have been nice to know beforehand. The longer I sat the more anxious I got; that was, until Nikki showed up holding a small suitcase and a garment bag. Placing the suitcase on the floor, she looked over to me and said, "Are you ready to be transformed?"

With a nod, I said, "Let's get this over with."

Standing beside her, I watched as she began taking things from the suitcase. With everything she had, I finally knew what I was being transformed into. Handing things to me to put on, I was slowly beginning to see the change myself. When Nikki handed me the final item to complete my disguise, I placed it on my head, tucking my hair underneath it.

With everything in place, I walked over to the full length mirror to see the new me. I couldn't believe what I saw. It was hard to believe that it was even me, I was looking at. If I didn't know better, the person I saw could have been my brother.

"Nikki, I look really good. Nobody will be able to recognize me," I said.

"That's the whole point, silly. Isabelle, I'd like you to meet Paul," she said with a giggle.

When I left the shop, everything that I had tried on was hidden away in a bridal gown garment bag underneath the gown itself. Nikki was pretty confident that Maxwell would be opening the bag to check its contents, but Victor would not, especially since it was bad luck to see the bride's gown before the wedding.

Just like she had suspected, Maxwell unzipped the bag and took a quick peek inside. Satisfied that it was only my wedding dress, he zipped the bag up and handed it to Peter to stow away in the trunk.

Before we headed to the palace, Peter was instructed to take Victor to his home near the palace. He had spent so much time at the palace, it hadn't even dawned on me that he had a place of his own. With a final kiss on my cheek, Victor was out of the car and out of my life forever. The minute the passenger door closed, Peter had the car in drive and exiting the estate of Victor 'Douche-bag' Walsh.

We were in front of the palace in minutes. Peter rounded the car to help me out while Maxwell exited the other side. Walking over to the trunk, Peter took the bag and followed me inside. We were up the marble steps as Maxwell entered the house.

"I think that Isabelle can manage the garment bag herself," he spat, looking directly at Peter.

With a nod of his head, Peter said, "Of course, sir."

God, how I couldn't wait until I was out of this place forever. Climbing up the remaining steps, my two wonderful bodyguards were already standing at my door. I knew that Nikki would be providing a distraction for me so I could get down the steps and to the kitchen. I only had a short time to change into my disguise and get there before they would see that I was no longer in my room.

The two men parted as I entered my room. I quickly began stripping off my clothing and changing into my disguise. I was thankful that Nikki helped me so that I would remember how to put everything on. There were so many steps that I needed to take and things that I needed to put on, it surprised me that it didn't weigh down the bag and make Maxwell more suspicious than he was.

Looking in the mirror, I was ready to go. I just needed to wait for Nikki to give me the signal. I only prayed that when she did, there would be no one else outside waiting for me.

CHAPTER TWENTY-EIGHT

Hawk

As I was waiting in the basement just on the other side of the secret door leading to the kitchen, I kept thinking about how beautiful Paige looked. Even though she looked pale, I figured that was normal for everything she had been through. I was just happy that she was alive and we were finally going to be together. Listening for any sound that was coming from the other side, I wanted to be prepared for Paige. I knew that she would be showing up any minute. I wanted to get as far away from this place as possible.

Just as I was about ready to check and see what was going on, I heard two women's voices. One of them I would know anywhere. It was my baby, Paige. Opening the cupboard door, I couldn't believe what I saw. I recognized Nikki, but Paige looked so much like a man, I had to look twice to make sure it was actually her. Stepping out into the open, I had to know for myself that it was really her. Pulling her body close to mine. I placed my lips on hers and parted them with my tongue. Other than the uncomfortable feeling of the mustache she was wearing on my lip, it was definitely her. Nobody could kiss the way she could.

"Come on, you guys, we need to get out of here before they figure out was is going on," Nikki whispered, pulling us from our embrace.

"Okay, okay," Paige snapped, pressing on her mustache to make sure it was still on securely.

I made sure that the two girls got through the secret door before me. Closing the cupboard door, I squeezed through the small area between the shelving and the door. Once through, I closed the door and secured it before removing the latch that would allow entrance from the other side. I wasn't sure where the other steps from the kitchen led, but if I had to guess, it was separate from this area of the basement.

The girls were waiting at the bottom of the steps until I could join them and show them the way out. Turning on the flashlight, I got in front of them and led them down the short hallway and then through the door to the main part of the dungeon. I could tell the musty smell of dampness was beginning to get to Paige as she started to fall behind. Stopping, I went over to where she was leaning up against the stone wall.

"Baby, are you okay?" I asked with concern.

"Yeah, I'll be okay. The smell down here is just making me nauseated," she confessed.

Taking her in my arms, I lifted her from the floor and carried her the rest of the way down the narrow hallway. Reaching the set of steps leading out of the dungeon, I set Paige down. Still holding on to her, I caressed her damp cheek and said quietly, "We're almost out, baby. Do you think you can climb the steps?"

With a nod of her head, she confirmed that she would be all right. Letting Nikki go first, I handed her the flashlight so she could guide us to the top of the steps. Once she opened the hidden door and Paige could breathe in the fresh air, she began to feel better. From the moment I saw her this morning, she didn't look well. I thought that it might have been from the ordeal, but this was something else.

Making our way across the lawn and to the front of the palace, I spotted two of the palace guards standing out front. There was no way that we were going to be able to get to the car with them standing so close. Our only option was to act like we belonged and pray they didn't find anything about us out of the ordinary. Taking my lead, Paige and Nikki followed behind me. When we got close enough, I pretended to be amused by something Nikki said.

"You got to be kidding, How the hell does that even happen?" I asked with no clue what she was going to say.

"Well, it's pretty simple," she began. "Oh, hey, guys. Are you done for the day?"

“Yeah, me and the wife have some pretty important plans for the evening, if you know what I mean,” the larger of the two men said.

“Gotcha. Well, have a good evening,” Nikki replied.

As we got inside the car, the two men waved goodbye to us. I couldn’t fucking believe that they didn’t question why a chauffeur, a servant, and a maintenance man would be out on the grounds this late in the evening. They didn’t even question where we were going. It was unbelievable how incredibly stupid they really were. Their stupidity just gave us a free ticket out of here. When we were far enough outside the gate, Paige removed her wig and her press-on mustache. Without her little get-up, she was even more beautiful. Taking the hand that she had resting on her lap, I lifted to my mouth and kissed it gently.

“It’s over, baby, you can finally go home,” I said softly.

With a tear in her eye, she said, “It isn’t, Hawk.

Eventually they are going to come after me. They may not have won this time, but I know my uncle, he will never give-up."

"Then we will just need to make sure that never happens," I vowed.

"You can't protect me all the time, Hawk. I need to let the people of Kierabali know what kind of men my uncle and Victor really are, and to do that I need to start being the person I really am, Princess Isabelle Moraco."

I knew she was right. She was a princess and I needed to start realizing that. Even though she would always be my Paige, I needed to call her Isabelle. Pulling out my cell, I called Peter and let him know of our change of plans. As much as he didn't like the idea of spending more time in Kierabali, he also agreed that Isabelle needed to take care of this once and for all.

~****~

As Isabelle stood in front of the podium at the

American Embassy, I couldn't help but be proud of this beautiful woman. She had been through so much over the past couple of weeks. When she told me what Victor did to her, I wanted to kill him, but killing him would be too good for him. Once Isabelle explained to the people what her uncle and Victor did, they would be spending most of their lives behind bars.

Looking into the crowd of people, I listened to the words Isabelle shared with them. The way she carried herself, she was a princess. Most of the women had tears in their eyes, while the men just bowed their heads down in regret. "So it is with great regret that I will be stepping down as Princess of Kierabali," Isabelle said sadly as she ended her speech.

As she turned and walked away, there was a shout from the crowd. "Princess, marry the man that you love, and rule Kierabali together."

Looking up at me, her face was filled with sorrow. I knew that she didn't want to be a princess, but I also knew that she didn't want to let her people down. Taking her by the hand, I lowered down to one knee and said to her so that everyone could hear. “Isabelle, I love you with all my being. I have never met a woman quite like you. You have changed me to be a better person. I would love nothing more than to be by your side forever. Will you marry me?”

Lowering herself to me, she choked out, “You want to marry me?”

“With all my heart,” I confessed.

“And you would be okay living in Kierabali as a prince, my prince?”

“Yeah.”

“Then yes, I will marry you.”

Her head lowered to mine and our lips met. I could hear the crowd going wild over her acceptance. Not only did they get their princess back, they also gained a man who loved this woman as much as they did.

Heading back inside the embassy, it finally dawned on me that I was going to be a prince. I didn't even know the first thing about being a prince. Dwelling on my own realization, I glanced over to Isabelle. God, she was beautiful. Looking back over to the crowd of people, I could see their joy as their cheering filled the air. I gave them a quick wave as I pulled her closer to me and gave her a tender kiss on the head. When she looked up at me with a blank stare, I knew then something was going on with her. I wrapped my arms around her as her body began going limp. With everything I had, I lifted her and carried her through the embassy doors.

It was when I was laying her on the couch just inside that I knew someone had gotten to her. The blood was so red as it spilled from her body. Frantically, I began to yell, "Help, somebody, please help!"

I did everything I was trained to do to help the bleeding stop. It just kept coming. Her eyes closed and my heart died.

~****~

As I was sitting in the chair, the events of the day began rushing in. All I could think about was the look on Isabelle's face. It was so empty. Like I had lost her forever. Looking over to Sly and Nikki, I could see that she was just as worried as I was. I was thankful that at least Sly was here with her. They had been getting quite close since this whole ordeal started. Lowering my head, I placed it in my hands. I closed my eyes and began to pray that Isabelle would be okay. That she wouldn't be taken away from me.

I was just about ready to find out what was going on with her when a doctor walked up to me. Standing, I faced him, ready to hear the critical news he had to share about Isabelle's condition.

"Mr. Talbott, I presume, from the news footage this morning," he said, holding out his hand to me.

"How is she?" I asked, not interested in the introduction.

"She's lost a lot of blood, but she and the baby will

be fine," he announced.

"Wait, what do you mean, 'the baby?'" I asked, confused.

"I take it you didn't know. When we checked her blood type to make sure we knew it, several other tests were run. Princess Isabelle is about four weeks pregnant."

"Wow, I wasn't expecting that," I said, still trying grasp what he just said.

"Well, I can understand that. If you like, you may see her, she should be in her private room by now. She might be a little groggy from the anesthesia," the doctor advised.

Walking down the hall to Isabelle's room, I still couldn't believe that she was pregnant. It would definitely explain the pale look she had and the queasiness she had at the palace. I wasn't even sure if I was ready to be a dad. I had stayed away from serious relationships for that very reason. The last thing that I wanted was to be like my dad.

As much as I wanted to forget about that part of my life, I knew that it would always be there. Sooner or later I knew that I would need to let Isabelle know about my childhood, especially now that she was going to be my wife.

Opening the door to her room, I saw the most gorgeous woman I had ever laid my eyes on. Even though her face still looked pale, her smile lit up her face when she saw me. “Hey, beautiful,” I said as I walked up to her.

“Hey,” she replied.

“How are you feeling?”

“A little tired.”

“That’s to be expected. Do you remember what happened?” I asked as I took a seat beside her.

“Yeah, someone shot me. Why, Hawk?” she muttered as her eyes began to well.

“Peter has a pretty good idea who it was, The cameras at the embassy will show who for sure.”

"Victor," she snapped.

"Yeah. Let's not talk about that now. We need to talk about something more important."

"The baby."

Interrupting our conversation. Peter tapped his hand against the glass window. Walking over to the bed, he stood beside me and asked, "Hey, you two, how's the mother-to-be?"

I had no idea that he knew. The only explanation was that Sly and Nikki must have told him. "We are fine," I answered.

"Well, I just wanted to check on Isabelle and let you guys know that Victor is being booked on charges of attempted murder. The cameras at the embassy got a perfect picture of him. Even though he wasn't amongst the crowd, the camera was angled such that it showed him across the street in one of the rooms."

“Well, that’s good news,” I stated, squeezing Isabelle’s hand.

“Got even better news for you. Maxwell was caught fleeing the country. We did some investigating on the picture you found of him and the other man exchanging briefcases. Turns out it was a payoff to have your parents killed. The money was used to put a device in the car that allowed someone to control the steering wheel. We located the man who developed the device. He said the exchange was to further his research on the product. Maxwell told him he wanted to help him develop it. In exchange for the prototype, Maxwell gave him money, saying it was an advance on the profit they would be making. It was the same device that was found in your parents’ car. Maxwell was responsible for their death. Long story short, he will be spending the rest of his days in jail.”

Looking over to Isabelle, I wasn’t surprised to find that she didn’t show any emotions. Based on the information she kept in the manila envelope, my guess was that she knew Maxwell was behind the death of her parents.

CHAPTER TWENTY-NINE

Isabelle

After Hawk and I talked about the baby it was very clear to me that he was scared to be a father. I couldn't understand why. He would be a wonderful dad. His compassion for people was evidence of that. Even while I was in the hospital, he made certain that I was being well cared for. He even went so far as to provide me with meals from a local restaurant. He claimed that he didn't want me eating the hospital food and that our baby needed the proper nutrition. It wasn't that the food at the hospital was bad. It was actually quite good, but he insisted it wasn't good enough for his girl.

Getting home and into my own bed was all that I wanted. Hawk had been instructing the staff what to do to prepare for my arrival at home. I had to laugh at the way he was fussing over me. He was definitely taking on the role of the new man of the house. When we got to my, or should I say our, new room, the bed had already been turned down. Being who he was, he insisted on carrying me up the steps. It didn't matter that I was perfectly capable of walking myself, he felt it necessary that I stayed off my feet. It wasn't like I was nine months pregnant.

Placing me on the bed, Hawk started helping me change into something that would be more comfortable. As he removed my top, I could see the desire he had in his eyes. With everything that had happened, the only contact that we had was a tender kiss here or there. I was so horny for this man that when my shirt came off, I tugged at the waistband of his jeans and pulled him closer. His head lowered and my lips were on his. I missed him so much, it felt like I was dying of thirst. I couldn't get enough of him. Grabbing the hem of his t-shirt, I yanked it over his head, exposing his hard muscles. I had never really taken a good look at him, but today was going to be different. Running my hand along his pecs and then down his sides, I stopped at the tattoo that was etched on his right side. Placing my finger over each word, I began reading them to myself, *'God Gives His Toughest Battles To His Strongest Soldiers.'* I wasn't sure what it meant exactly, Looking up at him, he knew what I was asking.

Sitting on the bed beside me, he took my hand and looked at me with uneasiness. "Isabelle, there is something you need to know about me."

"Does it have to do with the tattoo and scar it is hiding?" I asked, concerned.

"Yes, that and why I'm so afraid to be a dad," he replied.

"It's okay, Hawk. If this is too painful for you, you don't need to tell me," I stated.

"I do, Isabelle. You are going to be my wife and you need to know everything. I don't want to keep anything from you."

I looked up at Hawk, realizing how hard this was

going to be for him. Whatever he was about to tell me, I knew it wouldn't change the way I felt. Giving him my attention, I listened to what he had to say.

"My childhood wasn't the greatest. Matter of fact, it was the shittiest childhood that you could possibly imagine. I hated my dad. Every day I wished that he would just disappear from the face of the earth. I remember once when I was about twelve, me and my brother Drew were working on our bikes that we got at a garage sale down the block. The lady who had them didn't sell them and she didn't want to hold on to them, so she gave them to us for free. We were so excited. There wasn't anything wrong with them except that the chains needed to be adjusted. Anyway, when we got them home, we borrowed a screwdriver from my dad's tool box. Once we got the chains back on, we took the bikes for a spin. It was the greatest day of our lives, at least until we got back to the house." Hawk stood, running his hands through his hair, pacing the floor like he was about to explode with anger.

"Hawk, it's okay," I said, standing to comfort him.

Before I could touch him, he moved away to continue. "He was waiting for us in the garage. If we had just put everything back that we used, he wouldn't have done what he did. When we got back to the house, he was standing in the garage, just waiting for us. Drew was off his bike first. My dad didn't even give him a chance to put the kickstand down. Drew was thrown so far across the garage by my dad that when he landed I could hear his knee snap when he hit the concrete. Even though my dad was bigger than me, I went after him. All I could see was fire. My only regret was that I didn't kill him then. If it wasn't for the neighbor lady stopping over to see what was going on, I would have been in the same shape as my brother, if not worse. After he convinced the lady that everything was fine, he went inside the house and started on my mom."

"I'm so sorry, Hawk," I said as I began to cry.

"That's not even the worst of it." He started looking back at me. "After so many years of abuse, I was done. My dad wasn't going to ever hurt us again. This scar reminds me every day what he did to me and my mom. I almost died the day he came after me. I should have stabbed him in the back with that knife instead of throwing it at him. You should have seen the look on his face when he pulled it out of his neck. He came after me with such vengeance, I thought for sure I was going to die. The way he was holding that knife, he wanted me dead, only he didn't finish the job. He only got a part of me. It was the last time he would ever hurt any of us again, or so I thought. I think he got scared. He ran out of the house so fast, and left me and my mom there, me bleeding half to death and her beaten."

"What happened to him, Hawk?"

"He finally got what he had coming to him. He came back to the house about a week later, drunk off his ass. I was in my bedroom when I heard him arguing with my mom. I prayed that he would just leave, but he didn't. When I heard the sound of glass breaking, I knew something happened. My mom finally defended herself, after all this time, only it was too late. There was blood everywhere. I couldn't even recognize her face. She wasn't moving. I was so angry. Why did she let him beat her? I did the only thing I could. I took a piece of glass that was laying on the kitchen floor and went after him to finish this once and for all. My clothes were covered in his blood. The next day I left for the service and never looked back. For years I hid what really happened that day. He's where he should be, at the bottom of Boomer Lake. You're the only person I have ever told. Even my brother Drew doesn't know. As far as he knows, the bastard took off."

~****~

Hawk

As strong as I was all these years, the truth finally took hold of me. I fell to my knees and broke down. All the demons from my past were finally set free. My sweet angel was right there to help me keep them away. Kneeling beside me, she lifted my head and kissed me tenderly and with so much passion that my heart finally knew what true love was.

Picking her up and carrying her to the bed, I began worshiping my angel. The feel of her body beneath mine was how I wanted it to always be. Raising her hands above her head, I kissed her lips. Holding on to her wrists with one hand, I lowered the strap of her bra and gently placed a kiss on her shoulder. By lowering her strap, her taut nipple was exposed, waiting for me to consume it. Placing my month over the hard bud, I used my tongue to make circular movements around the peak before taking it fully between my lips, licking and sucking it gently. As I continue my assault on her nipple, I lowered my free hand down her silky skin and lowered the zipper on her jeans. The minute her bottom came off the bed, I was able to push them all the way down her legs and completely off her.

My hand found its place between her legs, where I could feel the wetness. Her warmth was all I needed to make my cock spring to life. Freeing her hands, I towered above her and removed the last of my clothes. She looked like heaven with her beautiful body ringed in white silk. Placing my hands on her hips, I lowered her soaked panties and took in her scent. Everything about her was perfect. With my body between her legs, I pushed them wider and began to consume her. I could hear the small moans of pleasure escape, letting me know just how much she was enjoying my play. Her enjoyment was nowhere near what she was doing to my cock. As badly as I wanted to enter her, I needed to taste her first. Slipping my tongue inside her vagina, I knew that this was indeed heaven. He juices began coating my tongue as the first blast of ecstasy filled my senses. Lapping up her juices, I moved up to her clit, where I found it swollen and ready for me. Circling and sucking, her body began to react as her back lifted from the bed. Lifting to my knees, I pulled her body closer and continue my assault on her wet pussy.

With another lap of my tongue on her clit, I placed my finger inside her tight channel, sending her reeling with another orgasm. When her cry for more sounded, I knew it was my turn. "Hawk, I need you inside me."

"What's the magic word, baby?" I asked

"Please," she begged.

Unable to tame down my own desire for this woman, I positioned my cock to her entrance and inched my way inside her wet pussy. The feel of her wrapped tight around my cock was a feeling like no other. I just wanted to plunge deeper and deeper inside her. I knew that I would need to take it slow. The best thing for me was enjoying every thrust as she pulled me further and further inside. Lowering my body over hers. I placed my head in the nape of her neck and breathed in her scent. With a whispered groan, I said, “I love Isabelle Moraco.” My control left and my seed spilled inside her.

Never would there be another woman for me. I found my heaven. My princess. My Isabelle.

About the Author

My passion for writing began a little over two years ago when I retired from a nine to five job. Even though I enjoyed working, I wanted something different. It was then that I decided that I wanted to write. Romance and passion is a topic that everyone desires in life, and it is for that reason I decided to write Erotic romances. Finding my niche as a romance writer has not only filled my heart, but also has kept me young. When I'm not writing, I like to spend time outside taking long walks and sipping wine under the stars.

I hope you found **Hawk** enjoyable to read. Please consider taking the time to share your thoughts and leave a review on the on-line bookstore. It would make the difference in helping another reader decide to read this and my upcoming books in the Jagged Edge Series.

To get up–to-date information on when the next Jagged Edge Series will be released click on the following link http://allong6.wix.com/allongbooks and add your information to my mailing list. There is also something extra for you when you join.

Coming Soon!!!!!!

Jagged Edge Series

Sly: Jagged Edge Series #4

Read all the books in the Jagged Edge Series

Hewitt: Jagged Edge Series #1

Cop: Jagged Edge Series #2

Hawk: Jagged Edge Series #3

Other books by A.L. Long

Next to Never: Shattered Innocence Trilogy

Next to Always: Shattered Innocence Trilogy, Book Two

Next to Forever: Shattered Innocence Trilogy, Book Three

To keep up with all the latest releases:

Twitter:

http://twitter.com/allong1963

Facebook:

http://www.facebook.com/ALLongbooks

Official Website:

http://www.allongbooks.com

Made in the USA
Charleston, SC
25 October 2016